First published in Great Britain by Purnell Books 1976.
Designed and produced by Intercontinental Book Productions
Reprinted 1988 by Macdonald & Co (Publishers) Ltd
under the Black Cat imprint

Macdonald & Co (Publishers) Ltd,
3rd Floor, Greater London House,
Hampstead Road, London NW1 7QX

a member of Maxwell Pergamon Publishing Corporation plc

ISBN 0-7481-0165-9

Printed in Czechoslovakia
52194

TALES
from
GRIMM
ANDERSEN
and
PERRAULT

Retold by Jane Carruth

BLACK CAT

Contents

Puss-in-Boots

THERE WAS once a poor miller who had three sons. He was so poor that when he died he left only his mill, his donkey and his cat.

"I'll take the mill," said the eldest son. "The mill is mine by rights."

"I'll take the donkey," said the second son. "With the donkey to carry loads, I can set up in business on my own."

"That leaves me with the cat," said the third and youngest son. "How is a cat going to help me to earn my living? What am I going to do?"

His two brothers were much too greedy and selfish to care, so the miller's youngest son took the cat and went off by himself to think out what he could do.

"I shall almost certainly starve to death," he said aloud, as he sat down under a tree. "Life is very unfair."

"I wouldn't say that," remarked the cat. "You could find me of great use if you would only trust me."

"What! Trust a cat to make my fortune," exclaimed the young man scornfully. "That's a very fine thing to ask me to do."

Now it didn't seem a bit strange to the miller's son that he should find himself talking to a cat. At the time of which I write, there were

7

quite a few talking animals around and the miller's son knew this. Besides he couldn't help remembering that his father's cat had been quite exceptionally clever in the way he had caught rats and mice.

"All I need," said the cat, after a short silence, "is a pair of high boots and a big sack. Give them to me and I promise that you will not be disappointed."

In spite of himself, the miller's youngest son began to believe in his cat. "I have very little money left," he said. "But I am willing to spend it on high boots for you although, I must admit, I cannot see why you want them. As for the sack, that is easily found."

"Never mind why I want the boots," said the cat. "Just wait and see."

As soon as the cat put on his fine new pair of red boots he seemed to grow more important, more certain of what he was going to do. "You wait here," he told his young master. "I'm going into the woods with my sack."

Puss-in-Boots wasted no time in the woods. First he filled his sack with bran and lettuce. Then he looped a long string around the neck of the sack so that he could close it whenever he wished. When this was done to his satisfaction, he lay down, the string in his paw, and pretended to be dead.

Now it is a well known fact that rabbits are very fond of lettuce and bran and, before long, a plump young rabbit hopped up to the sack. It smelt the bran and caught a glimpse of the tempting lettuce. Puss held the string firmly as the silly rabbit hopped inside the sack. And that was the end of the foolish young rabbit! Puss pulled the string, closed the sack's neck and pounced on his prisoner.

Well satisfied with his morning's work, Puss-in-Boots set off at once for the King's palace. So important did he look in his shining high boots that he was taken straight away to the King.

"A gift, Your Majesty," said Puss-in-Boots, without wasting words. "A gift from my most gracious and noble master, the Marquis of Carabas." This was the grand-sounding name that Puss had invented for the miller's son as he left the woods.

Now the King, as Puss knew, was extremely fond of rabbit pie and when he saw the plump young rabbit, he could hardly hide his royal pleasure. He coughed and his eyes twinkled. "Ahem!" he said at last, knowing that a king should not appear too pleased at receiving a present. "I am very grateful to your master, the – ahem – the Marquis of . . ."

"Carabas," said Puss firmly. "The Marquis of Carabas."

"Indeed yes," said the King. "The Marquis of Carabas. Yes, well, I shall certainly remember that name."

9

Puss-in-Boots, in fact, gave the King no chance to forget it for the very next morning he turned up at the palace with a pair of very fine wood pigeons; and the day after, with a plump pheasant.

By the end of the week, the King had eaten rabbit and pigeon pie to his heart's content and had almost begun to think of the Marquis of Carabas as a friend.

"I must meet your master soon," he said to Puss, when next the cat visited the palace. "I should very much like to thank him in person for so many fine gifts."

This was all Puss-in-Boots had been waiting to hear. He ran straight back to his master who, by this time, was extremely dirty and shabby though he always ate well, thanks to Puss.

"You must bathe in the river tomorrow at a certain hour," Puss told the young man. "Just do as I say and all will be well."

"I don't see why I should," grumbled the miller's son. "The water is cold at this time of the year and besides I have never enjoyed swimming."

"Never mind that," said Puss briskly. "I'll show you the exact spot where you must enter the river when the time comes."

By now, of course, the miller's son knew that Puss-in-Boots was up to something and could only hope that plans were underway to make his fortune. "Very well," he agreed. "I'll do what you ask."

The next morning Puss took his master to a spot on the riverside which was not far from the road. Only the week before Puss-in-Boots had learnt from some of the palace servants that the King and his charming daughter were in the habit of driving along this road in their carriage, and he had made his plans accordingly.

As soon as his master was undressed, Puss hid the ragged bundle of clothes under a big stone. Then he pushed him into the water. And then, down the road at a fine rattling pace came the King's carriage, and Puss began to shout at the top of his voice, "Help! Help! My master, the Marquis of Carabas, is drowning!"

So loudly and desperately did Puss shout that the King's attention was immediately attracted. "Stop!" he called to his coachman. "I know that name!" Then he saw Puss-in-Boots, and the cat pointed to the young man in midstream.

"My coachman will have him out of the water in a trice," the King assured Puss.

As the coachman somewhat unwillingly went to the rescue, Puss hastily whispered in the King's ear. "All my master's beautiful clothes

have been stolen," he told him. "Could you possibly have a new suit sent from the palace?"

"Yes indeed!" declared the King. "That is the least I can do."

When the miller's son was finally dressed in one of the King's own suits he looked very handsome indeed. So handsome, in fact, that the Princess, who had sat silent for all this time, gave him a very gracious smile and invited him to join her in the royal carriage.

"This is the noble Marquis of Carabas, my dear," said the King, as he too settled himself in the carriage. "He has sent us many fine gifts over the past weeks."

The miller's son heard this with great astonishment but was clever

enough to hide his surprise. Besides, the Princess was so very lovely that he just wanted to sit close to her forever.

Meanwhile, Puss was speeding down the road in his high boots. Soon he was ahead of the King's carriage and when he came upon some peasants working in a rich, golden meadow he stopped.

"Listen, my good fellows," he shouted. "In a few minutes the King's carriage will pass this way. If you do not tell him that this rich meadow and all the land surrounding it belongs to the Marquis of Carabas, I will have you chopped into little pieces . . ."

Puss-in-Boots looked and sounded so fierce that the peasants touched their caps and said, "We'll do as you say."

With a final scowl and a warning, Puss sped on his way for already he could hear the sound of horses' hooves behind him. Almost before he had rounded the next bend in the road, the King's carriage had reached the meadow.

Now the King was a greedy King and the sight of such a splendid golden meadow made him curious as to its owner.

"The Marquis of Carabas owns this meadow and all the land surrounding it," the peasants said in answer to the King's question.

"Indeed!" exclaimed the King, and he smiled in a very friendly way at the miller's son.

Running as fast as he could, Puss was able to keep ahead of the royal carriage. Whenever he saw a particularly rich field of crops or a well wooded piece of land he stopped. He always said the same thing to the peasants working close by.

"If you do not tell the King that all this land belongs to the Marquis of Carabas," he warned, "I will have you chopped into little pieces . . ."

In this way, clever Puss made certain that the King would soon

think that his master was one of the richest young men in his kingdom. But there was still more work to be done. He must find a castle. The only castle Puss-in-Boots had heard about belonged to an ogre who was also a magician.

When Puss reached the ogre's castle, he found him preparing for a banquet. "Well, what do you want?" demanded the ogre, in an unfriendly way.

"I have heard that you have marvellous powers," Puss said, bowing very low.

This pleased the ogre. "That's true," he admitted. "Marvellous powers – you never said a truer word."

"That's why I've come to see you," said Puss. "I – I just wanted to look at you."

"Well, that's a fine thing!" roared the ogre, suddenly very friendly. "That's what I call fame!"

"Of course you are famous, Sir Ogre," said Puss humbly. "You're so famous that I just had to pay you a visit. Do you know that some people say you can change yourself into any animal shape you choose?"

"So I can!" boasted the ogre. "You name the animal and I'll show you . . ."

"Even a lion?" asked Puss, his voice full of admiration.

"Even a lion!" roared the ogre, and, in a moment, Puss-in-Boots found himself face to face with a snarling lion. He got such a fright that he jumped, trembling, onto the window sill.

"That's – that's really wonderful, Sir Ogre," he squeaked. "But I suppose it's fairly easy for an ogre to change into such a huge creature as a lion?"

"It's no harder than changing into a tiger," said the ogre, when he was himself again.

"Ah, yes, well a tiger is much the same size as a lion," said Puss, jumping down from the ledge. "But how about something really small – well, like a . . . ." he stopped.

"I see what you mean!" laughed the ogre. "You think a big fellow like me can't make myself into a tiny creature, is that it?"

"Well, no, of course not," said Puss, but somehow he managed to look as if he didn't quite believe that the ogre could turn himself into something really small.

"You name the animal!" boasted the ogre, more than ever anxious to show off his powers.

"Well, the smallest creature I can think of is a mouse," said Puss.

15

"Watch!" cried the ogre, and with that he changed himself into a small brown mouse.

That was the moment Puss had been waiting for. With a snarl and a pounce he flattened the mouse on the floor and then ate it. That was the end of the ogre and certainly from Puss-in-Boot's point of view it happened not a moment too soon. He had only just time to rush up to the castle gates and be standing there as the royal carriage appeared.

"Upon my soul!" exclaimed the King. "There's Puss-in-Boots!"

"Welcome, Your Majesty, to the castle of my master the Marquis of Carabas," cried Puss, as the carriage stopped.

"So this splendid castle is yours!" exclaimed the King to the miller's son, as he helped the Princess to the ground. "Remarkably fine!"

The miller's son was by this time so deeply in love with the beautiful Princess that he was quite unable to say anything . . . which was just as well.

Puss-in-Boots led the small party into the banqueting room where the table was already, most fortunately, laid and the King's eyes sparkled at the sight of the gold plates and so many crystal goblets. "I don't know your feelings, young man," he said, turning to the miller's son. "But if, as it would seem, you have fallen in love with my daughter and wish to marry her, I won't stand in your way."

"If the Princess will have me," replied the miller's son, finding his tongue at last, "I shall be the happiest man in your kingdom."

"I will," cried the Princess, who was one of those girls who makes up her mind very quickly. "I haven't found anyone I like better."

So there and then, before they sat down at table, the wedding was arranged and there was no one more delighted than Puss himself.

After the wedding, which was held the very next day, Puss, at his own request, was given a new and exceedingly costly pair of high boots and a simply gorgeous outfit to match them.

In the eyes of his master, at least, nothing was too good for Puss-in-Boots!

The Proud Beetle

ONCE UPON a time there lived an Emperor. Now this Emperor had a very favourite horse. He was indeed a very noble creature with big bright eyes and a mane that hung over his neck like a veil. He had served his master well in battle and more than once had helped to save his life in the thick of the fighting. To show his affection and appreciation the Emperor had had shoes of pure gold put on the horse's feet.

Now all this and much more the horse had many times explained to a large black Beetle that shared his royal stable.

"I don't care what you say," the Beetle remarked finally. "I share your stable and I should have golden shoes just like you." And, with that, he went to the blacksmith to ask for them.

"Don't you know why the Emperor's horse is given golden shoes?" asked the smith.

"I suppose I do," said the Beetle. "But I consider myself as good as the horse." And he stretched out his six thin legs.

"Be off with you," cried the blacksmith. "Away! Shoo!"

The Beetle flew round his head, saying, "Very well, I'll leave the stable for ever and find a place where I shall be honoured as one who knows the Emperor."

After flying a short while, the Beetle presently found himself in a beautiful flower garden, filled with the scent of roses and lavender.

"Welcome to our garden," said a dainty little ladybird. "It is very pretty here," and she turned round so that the Beetle could admire her red and black spotted coat.

"Do you think so!" exclaimed the Beetle. "I am used to a much better place than this!" And he flew on.

After a little while he came upon a caterpillar crawling along under the shadow of a huge cabbage leaf.

"Well, hello!" said the caterpillar, as the Beetle flew down to look at him. "Have you come to stay? It's quite delightful here and very sheltered. If you stay long enough you'll have the pleasure of seeing me turn into a butterfly."

"I don't want to see anything of the kind," said the Beetle rudely. "I'll have you know that I have come out of the Emperor's stable and his favourite horse has to wear my golden shoes when I have finished with them," the Beetle lied. "Really, I don't know why I waste time talking to a common caterpillar." And away he flew.

Soon afterwards, the Beetle dropped down to the grass and, tired after so much exercise, he fell fast asleep. As he slept it began to rain. The heavy shower not only soaked his wings but sent him tumbling over and over in the wet grass. Goodness knows what would have become of the proud Beetle if he had not managed to find his six feet again. When he did, he rubbed the water out of his eyes and crawled into the sheltering folds of a linen sheet that had blown on to the ground. Very much out of temper, he lay perfectly still until the rain stopped.

When, at last, he felt strong enough to start his journey again, he found two frogs sitting close together on top of the sheet, their bright eyes shining with pleasure. "Wonderful weather this!" one of them said to the Beetle. "All this rain is so good for our skins. We love it!"

"I hate it," said the Beetle disagreeably. "In my royal stable at home it is warm and comfortable and not the least bit damp. The Emperor sees to everything. Did you know that his favourite horse has to wear my cast-off golden shoes?"

The frogs let out a few stupid croaks at this and the Beetle, certain that they were laughing at him, flew off in an angry way. "I must find a really snug dung-heap," he told himself, "where I can rest for a while." But although he flew round the garden once or twice he could not find a likely dung-heap. Instead, he came upon a ditch that the palace

18

gardeners had recently dug and there, sitting on the rich brown mud,
were several other beetles.

"We are very happy and content here," they told him, as he flew
down to join them. "It is true it is not quite as good as a dung-heap,
but we mustn't complain."

"I come from the Emperor's stable," boasted the Beetle. "I was born there with golden shoes on my feet. I don't wear them now because I am on a secret mission for the Emperor."

The Beetle spoke with such pride and looked so important that the mother of three young girl beetles hurriedly pushed them forward so that the Beetle would notice them. "If you are thinking of settling down," she said, "I have three fine daughters still unmarried."

"They are certainly very pretty and quite as good-looking as the females in the stables," admitted the Beetle, looking at the youngest.

"Then you will take one of them for your wife?" asked the mother beetle hopefully. "The wedding can be arranged very quickly."

"I will," said the Beetle. "I'll take your youngest. One day she can come back with me to the stable on a visit and I'll show her off to the Emperor's favourite horse."

So the Beetle got married and for a little while was content. However, he soon began to find that as a husband he was expected to perform a number of humble tasks. This was too much for his pride and, by the end of the week, he left the ditch when his young wife was busy talking to her mother, and never went back.

By a great stroke of good fortune, the Beetle came, almost immediately, upon one of the Emperor's hothouses and finding the window open, flew inside. Here he felt immediately at home and settled down in the dark warm earth of one of the hot beds. Almost at once he fell fast asleep, when he dreamt that he was wearing the golden shoes that had once belonged to the Emperor's favourite horse. Most of his dream, however, was taken up with his search for two more golden shoes for, of course, the horse had need of only four while he required six.

When the Beetle awoke he began crawling about in the earth, thinking what a wonderful place the hothouse was and how presently he would sample some of the big-leafed plants that were everywhere. Suddenly, and to his great alarm, a hand seized him and rolled him over. The Beetle's six legs waved in the air and the little boy who had found him, laughed aloud. He was the gardener's son and he liked the hothouse as much as the Beetle did.

"Look what we have here," he said to his friend, who had followed him inside. "A beetle – a big, fat black shining beetle. Let's have some fun with him."

"Don't hurt him!" said his friend, who was a sensible boy.

"Of course not," said the gardener's son. "We'll just send him on a journey."

"That suits me very well," thought the Beetle, when he heard this. "It will save me the bother of flying."

The boys ran down to the lake and put the Beetle in an old broken wooden shoe. They used a thin stick for a mast and bound the Beetle to it with woollen thread.

"Now I'm a sailor," the Beetle told himself proudly, as the boat floated away over the water. "What a story I'll have to tell that horse when I choose to visit him."

But the boys did not mean the Beetle to sail away out of their lives. Laughing and shouting they waded into the lake and brought the boat back to shore so that they could send it out again on a different course. If you think this was cruel you are perfectly correct and soon the gardener's boy grew quite ashamed of himself. He bent down to set the Beetle free and tumbled into the water. Now the boy was in trouble himself and likely enough to get a beating from his father. His friend said, "It serves you right!" And ran off.

Meanwhile, the boat was drifting away into the middle of the lake and the Beetle was just beginning to wonder what could be the end of his adventure, when a dragonfly came whirring over his head.

"Beautiful weather," said the dragonfly. "I'll rest here for a minute and enjoy the sunshine. Are you having a nice time?"

"I don't think I am," said the Beetle. "I'm not exactly free to fly away when it suits me."

"Well, I am!" said the dragonfly, and off he went.

"The world does not deserve me," the Beetle told himself, as he watched the dragonfly go. "I come from the Emperor's stable and I am given no honour. Well, I have my pride. I will not be content until the world accepts me for what I am."

The old wooden shoe drifted on and on, over the lake until the Beetle began to wonder at last what was to become of him. "Perhaps it is all over for me," he thought. "If I had been given my golden shoes in the first place I would have stayed in the stable and been equal to that horse."

But it was not over for the Beetle. Two girls were rowing on the lake. They saw the Beetle's boat and they saw the Beetle.

"Look at that old wooden shoe sailing along," said one.

"And the little beetle bound to its mast," said the other. "Let's row over and set the Beetle free."

One of the girls had a small pair of scissors in her pocket and with these she cut the woollen thread that kept the Beetle prisoner. Picking him up, she held him gently in her hand while her friend rowed ashore. Once there, they set the Beetle free. Up, up he flew and then down through the open door of a long, low, building. Can you guess where he landed? He was back in the stable and clinging to the beautiful mane of the Emperor's favourite horse.

"Now, is this not very extraordinary?" the Beetle cried, when he felt stronger. "Here I am sitting on the Emperor's horse just like the Emperor himself! It is quite clear to me now why the horse was given his golden shoes. He is wearing them in my honour. I am equal to the Emperor in importance.''

And with a deep sigh of happiness, he closed his eyes in well-earned sleep.

Snow-White and Rose-Red

ONCE UPON a time there was a poor widow who had a little
cottage at the edge of a forest. Her greatest joy was two rose
trees, one white and the other red, which grew in a small patch
of garden. She named her two daughters after the rose trees, Snow-
White and Rose-Red. Snow-White was quiet and gentle and helped
a great deal in the house while Rose-Red was always gay and liked
nothing better than to chase through the forest on sunny days.

But although the sisters were different, as sisters so often are, they
were very close friends and were nearly always together. They had
explored the forest so often that they were never afraid to go there on
their own and sometimes the little rabbits would come and eat out
of their hands.

In the summer, the girls would fill their basket with berries and talk
to the shy little forest creatures. But in the winter, when the snow was
on the ground, their mother would bolt the door, and call them over to
sit by the fire. Then, out would come her spectacles and Snow-White
would give her the big book of stories and legends that they all loved.
As they settled on a rug at their mother's feet, their pet deer would lie
down beside them just as if he, too, wanted to hear a story.

One night, as they sat together round the fire, there was a loud knock at the door. "Go quickly, Rose-Red," said her mother, looking up from her book. "Some poor traveller must have lost his way in the snow."

When Rose-Red opened the door, there was a huge black bear, who thrust his head forward and said, "Will you let me come in? I won't do you any harm and I am nearly frozen to death."

Rose-Red screamed in fright and tried to shut the door, but her mother called out, "Let the poor bear come in, Rose-Red. You heard what he said. We cannot turn away any living thing on a night like this."

So Rose-Red opened the door wide and the bear stepped into the cottage. He stood on the mat, looking quite enormous in the tiny room. "Will one of you kindly brush the snow from my back?" he said. And, half-ashamed that she should have been so frightened, Rose-Red did as he asked.

Then Snow-White made a place for him beside the fire, and her mother said, "You may stay here as long as you want to. You are welcome to come as often as you wish during these hard cold months of winter."

There was no more reading from the book of stories that night for although the bear said very little, he allowed the girls to tug at his fur and pretend to roll him on his back. And, soon, even the timid deer was joining in the fun.

When it was time for bed, the widow said, "Stay here by the hearth where you will be nice and warm," and the bear nodded in a friendly way before stretching himself out on the rug.

In the morning, when Rose-Red ran into the kitchen, he was gone, but he returned early the next evening and once again they spent a happy time together.

All through the cold winter, the bear never missed a night and the girls grew to look forward to the evenings and to hearing his knock. But when spring came and the little birds welcomed Snow-White and Rose-Red into the forest with their songs, the bear said, "I must leave you now until winter comes again."

"Where will you go?" Snow-White asked sadly, scarcely able to hide her tears. "We shall miss you so much."

"Deep into the forest," the bear told her. "My treasure lies hidden there and I must guard it. In the winter the ground is hard and the wicked dwarfs who would steal it cannot dig it up. But in the spring and summer the earth is soft and the dwarfs dig deep burrows and steal all they can lay their hands on."

How sad Snow-White and Rose-Red were to see the bear go and as they watched him trot away, Snow-White said, "It won't be the same now that he has gone."

Some days later, their mother asked them to go into the forest and gather some wood. "You will enjoy the sunshine," she said, "and perhaps it will help you to forget the bear."

As the two girls wandered along the paths, searching for sticks, they were suddenly surprised to see an odd little man whose long white beard was caught in the branches of a tree.

"Look!" whispered Rose-Red, "the tree must have fallen and trapped that funny little man by his beard."

The little man, his face all lined and wrinkled like a crab-apple, was struggling desperately to free himself and when he caught sight of the girls, he screamed, "Fools! Idiots! Don't stand gaping! Help me, can't you?"

At this, the sisters bent down, took hold of the Dwarf's tunic and began to pull. But no matter how they tugged and pulled they could not free him. At last Snow-White took a pair of small scissors out of

her pocket. "It won't hurt," she said, and snip, snip, she cut off the end of his beard. "There!" she said, "now you are free."

If you are thinking that the Dwarf was grateful, you couldn't be more wrong. "Ruined! Ruined!" he screeched, hopping up and down holding his beard. "You've ruined my handsome white beard." And with a fierce scowl, he ran to a sack, which was filled with gold, threw it over his shoulder and stumped off into the bushes.

"Well!" said Rose-Red. "What a horrid little man! I wish we had left him alone."

"We had to help him," said Snow-White. "But I think he might have thanked us. Let's forget him and collect some wood."

But the girls were to see the Dwarf again much sooner than they expected. The very next day they went down to the stream to feed the wild ducks, and there he was again.

"It's the Dwarf!" Snow-White whispered, taking her sister's arm. "And he's in trouble again."

"So I see," said Rose-Red, although she didn't sound very sorry. "It looks as if he has been fishing and his beard has got tangled up in his line. Well, I don't care. This time I refuse to help."

But gentle Snow-White murmured, "I think we should try to get him free or else that huge fish at the end of his line is going to pull him right into the water."

"Then he'll get a soaking, that's all," said Rose-Red, rather heartlessly. The little man was in great danger of being pulled into the water, as she spoke, and he was now clinging desperately to some tall reeds. When he glanced up and saw the girls, he screamed, "Help! Help! Help me you – you idiots! Don't stand there like stupid sheep. Do something."

Snow-White and Rose-Red did as he said. They ran to him, and Snow-White took hold of his tunic and pulled. What a tug of war it was for the big fish was pulling too, to get free! But no matter how hard she tugged and pulled she could not free the little man. His beautiful white beard was so tangled up with the fishing-rod that nothing, it seemed, could move it.

"You know what you're going to have to do," said Rose-Red, as Snow-White, all out of breath, sank to the ground. "You're going to have to use your scissors again."

"I suppose I must," Snow-White said. And scrambling to her feet, she took out her scissors. Snip, snip, snip! Off came some more of the little man's beard.

The Dwarf was almost speechless with rage when he saw part of his precious beard lying on the grass. "You've spoilt my beard again!" he spluttered. "You did it on purpose!"

"We did not," cried Rose-Red. But the little man, his face all red and wrinkled with hate, glared at her so hard that she stopped, feeling suddenly frightened. Then, without another word, he went to a big stone and picked up a sack that lay behind it. As he heaved it up to his

shoulder, a handful of gleaming pearls fell out of it. Then he disappeared into the bushes.

Snow-White and Rose-Red said nothing of the unpleasant little Dwarf to their mother because they were afraid she might say they couldn't go into the forest.

"It isn't as if he could do us any real harm," said Rose-Red as they talked about him. "He is just horrid and ungrateful."

"I think he is wicked," said Snow-White, with a shiver. "And what is he doing with the gold and pearls? I don't believe they belong to him."

They were still talking about the Dwarf when their mother came into the kitchen the next day and asked them to go down to the village to buy some needles and cotton.

Pleased at the chance of doing something for her and going outdoors, Snow-White and Rose-Red ran off through the forest for that was the shortest way to the village. While they were still among the trees, they noticed a huge eagle soaring above their heads. Suddenly it swooped downwards and Rose-Red cried, "Oh dear, it must have seen

31

something to eat. I hope it isn't after one of our little rabbit friends."

Then a familiar cry reached their ears, "Help! Help! Help me!"

"It's the Dwarf!" Snow-White cried, and she began to run. "The eagle must be after the little man."

The girls rushed into a clearing in the forest just as the big bird dropped down on the Dwarf, and was preparing to carry him off. With a cry of horror, Rose-Red grabbed the little man's feet while her sister took hold of his beard. The eagle had no intention of giving up its prey too easily and the dwarf screamed in pain and terror as he was lifted off the ground. But the sisters hung on with all their strength until the bird gave up the struggle and flew away.

No sooner had the Dwarf recovered from his fright than he shook his fist angrily at Snow-White and Rose-Red. "Fools! Idiots!" he shouted at them. "You have torn my coat. My head aches with the way you pulled at my beard. Couldn't you take more care?" And he ran off picking up a sack that lay half-hidden in the long grass.

"I don't care," said Snow-White. "I'm glad we saved him. Just imagine being carried off by an eagle!"

On their way back from the village, the sisters were surprised to come upon the little man again. Rose-Red pulled her sister behind a tree and they watched as he emptied one of his sacks on a flat stone. The precious stones shone like tiny stars in the bright sunlight and Snow-White let out a gasp of amazement.

The Dwarf whirled round immediately and saw them. "Spies! Robbers!" he shouted in sudden fury. "Be off with you!"

"We are not spies and we don't want anything from you," said Rose-Red, stepping out from behind the tree and facing the angry Dwarf. "So please don't shout at us."

"We have saved your life three times," said Snow-White, joining her sister. "And you haven't even thanked us."

Her words sent the little man into such a rage that he began hopping up and down, shaking his fist, and shouting at them to leave him alone. No wonder he failed to see the huge black bear come padding up behind him! When he did, it was too late to turn and run for the bear had grasped him in his broad paw. When he found himself a prisoner, the Dwarf's angry shouting changed to a pathetic whine.

"Spare me, Lord Bear," he whimpered. "I meant no harm. Take these precious stones – they are worth a fortune. And take those stupid girls there. They'll make you a much tastier meal than me."

Snow-White and Rose-Red clung to each other in terror for they

did not recognise the big black bear as their friend and playmate of the long winter evenings.

Still holding the Dwarf in his paw, the bear turned to them, saying "I am your friend. Don't you know me?" As he spoke, he dropped his captive to the ground, killing him with a single blow from his great paw. Instantly, something strange and wonderful happened. In place of the bear stood a handsome young man, clothed in a suit of gold.

Snow-White and Rose-Red stared in amazement until the young man said, "The death of that wicked Dwarf has set me free from the spell he cast upon me. Out of greed he condemned me to wander through this forest in the shape of a bear so that he might rob me of my treasure. Now I am free and able to return to my father's palace."

"Will – will you not return first to our cottage," said Snow-White shyly. "Our mother would love to see you."

"Most certainly," said the young Prince, "for there is something very important that I must ask her."

Can you guess what it was? The Prince had long ago fallen in love with the gentle Snow-White and wished to ask her mother for permission to make her his wife. Of course this was gladly given. And after they were happily married, Snow-White told her sister and mother that she wanted them to live with her in the splendid palace. This they gladly consented to do, and great was the mother's joy when the Prince himself planted two rose trees in the royal gardens, one white and the other red, just like the ones that had once bloomed in her tiny cottage garden.

The Three Wishes

ONCE UPON a time there was a poor woodcutter who was forever complaining. It is true that although he worked extremely hard he had very little to show for it. He had a small cottage at the edge of a forest which he could call his own and he had a wife.

One day this woodcutter was out in the forest felling trees. As they came crashing to the ground, he muttered aloud, "Work, work, work! Nothing but work! It's not fair, I tell you, it's not fair!"

Now the more the woodcutter grumbled the less he felt like working and, at last, he threw his axe down on the ground, ready to give up altogether. As he did so, there was a brilliant flash of lightning and a mighty clap of thunder and there, towering over him, was the great god of the heavens, Jupiter himself.

"If-if I-I have s-said anything to offend you –" the poor woodcutter began to stammer, "I r-really d-didn't mean to."

"I have heard your complaints," thundered the god, "and I have appeared before you to grant you three wishes. Think long and carefully before you make them for they will be granted the very instant they are made."

35

Jupiter vanished before the woodcutter had time to gather his his senses but when at last he realised the implication of the words the god had spoken, he gave a great shout of joy and ran, helter-skelter, to his cottage to tell his wife.

"Our fortunes are made," he cried, as he burst into the cottage. "Wife, wife where are you? I've got news for you!"

His wife came running and the woodcutter gasped, "Heap logs on the fire. Bring out the wine. We're going to be rich beyond our dreams."

Almost as excited as her husband, his wife Hannah put logs on the fire and brought out the wine she had been keeping for Christmas. When this was done, she sat down opposite her husband and begged him to tell her the good news.

"The great god, Jupiter, has spoken to me," her husband began, trying to keep his voice low and matter of fact. "I've just met him in the forest."

"Heavens above!" cried his wife, bitterly disappointed. "What nonsense is this? As if life isn't hard enough! Now I've got a madman for a husband."

"I'm not mad," said the woodcutter. "Listen, Hannah! While I was out in the forest just now Jupiter himself really did appear before me. There was this bright flash of lightning and clap of thunder – and there he was. I tell you my legs turned to jelly at the sight of him. But I stood up to him like a man. . ."

"I can imagine!" said his wife scornfully. "Well, what did he have to say to you?"

"He-er-praised me for my hard work," said her husband slyly. "And then he gave me three wishes."

Her husband spoke in such an earnest manner that in spite of herself

Hannah began to believe him. She poured him out a glass of wine and begged him to continue.

"Three wishes," repeated her husband. "We can ask for anything we like. Of course, we'll ask for money, and maybe a new house. . ."

"And I could have a diamond ring," interrupted Hannah, quite carried away, "and a carriage and a coat with real fur. . ."

"I said *three* wishes!" laughed her husband, as he warmed his hands at the fire. "We mustn't rush into them. We must talk about our wishes quietly and thoughtfully. What do you say we both think about them for the rest of the day and wish tomorrow?"

"You're right, husband," said the wife. "You speak with true wisdom. Let me fetch your slippers and fill your pipe."

At peace with the world, the woodcutter put on his slippers, leant back in his chair and remarked, "You know, Hannah, I wish we had a string of fat sausages cooking in the pan to eat as we drink this wine. . ."

No sooner had he spoken, than to his immense surprise, he saw a snake-like string of sausages moving towards him across the floor.

Hannah cried out, more in anger than fear, for being more quick-witted than her husband, she realised what had happened.

"Fool!" she screamed. "Idiot! You have thrown away one of our precious wishes. Money! A diamond ring! Anything – we could have had anything with that wish, and all you give us is a string of sausages. . ."

The poor woodcutter bowed his head under her flood of angry words. "You speak truly, wife," he mumbled. "All right, I have thrown away one of the three wishes."

His wife, however, refused to be silenced. "Can there be another fool as big as you?" she stormed. "Ass, donkey, hopeless imbecile! It's a pity I ever married you."

Stung into anger by her harsh words, the woodcutter got up from his chair and shouted. "Hold your tongue, woman! Upon my soul,

37

I wish that string of sausages was dangling from your nose. It might keep your mouth shut. . ."

No sooner had he spoken than the sausages, in an instant, had fastened themselves on to his wife's nose. The sight was so comical that the woodcutter burst out laughing. "Ho, ho!" he chortled. "Well, that's a fine way to stop a woman's mouth from opening too wide. . ."

Poor Hannah began to weep silently and, at the sight of her tears, the woodcutter no longer found her so funny. Indeed, he began to rather miserable himself. "I'm sorry, Hannah," he said at last. "That's our second wish gone, and nothing to show for it – unless you count these sausages. . ."

For a moment, he looked at her thoughtfully. Then he remembered all the good times they had enjoyed together when they were young. No, he couldn't leave her like that for the rest of her days.

"It's like this, Hannah," he began slowly. "You and I can hide ourselves away for the rest of our lives for I'm not sure I would care to be seen in high society with a wife who carries a string of sausages at the end of her nose – or," he paused unkindly. And his wife sobbed louder than ever. "Or," he repeated, "I can use up my third and last wish to make these sausages disappear. What shall I do?"

Hannah's eyes were so pleading that her husband stopped teasing her. With a sigh that echoed round the room, he said, slowly, "I wish, I wish that those sausages would go back where they came from."

So that was the end of the woodcutter's dreams. He had wasted his three wishes. Never again would he dare to grumble that life was unfair for he had had his wonderful chance and thrown it away. But this much can be said. Hannah was so grateful to be herself again that she stopped scolding her husband and took much better care of him.

Hansel and Gretel

THERE WAS once a poor woodcutter who was blessed with two loving children – a boy called Hansel and a girl called Gretel. When their own dear mother died, the woodcutter married again and this time he chose a wife who was neither loving nor gentle.

The woodcutter worked hard but soon he found he could no longer sell his wood in the market. Worse still, his savings were dwindling.

"What shall we do, wife?" he groaned, as they faced each other over the kitchen table. "My savings are gone and there is scarcely enough food in the house to feed you and the children."

"Then we must rid ourselves of the children," said his wife, after no more than a moment's thought. "Without them we could manage quite well. Why, Hansel eats as much as you do."

The woodcutter could scarcely believe his ears when he heard this, but his wife was determined. She nagged and scolded him, and in the evening, when Hansel and Gretel had gone upstairs to bed, she began all over again.

"You must take them into the forest early in the morning and leave them there," she said. "It's the only sensible thing to do. I am not willing to starve on their account."

In vain, her husband told her that he loved his children and that he

39

would rather die than do them harm. His wife refused to listen and became so angry that her voice got louder and louder. The noise of the shouting woke Hansel, so he climbed out of bed and tip-toed to the top of the stairs. As he stood there, quiet as a mouse, he heard his stepmother say, "Then it's settled. Tomorrow we take them into the forest and leave them there."

Hansel crept back to his little bed and lay there, wide awake, until at last Gretel crept in beside him. "I'm so hungry," she whispered, "I can't sleep, and besides I thought I heard our stepmother shouting."

Then Hansel told her what their fate was to be in the morning. "But take heart, little sister," he went on. "I've thought up a plan already.

As soon as the house is quiet, I'm going down into the garden to fill my pockets with shining white pebbles."

The moon was shining so brightly that the pebbles looked like real silver pennies as Hansel bent down and picked them up. He stuffed his pockets until they were bulging. Then he went back indoors and closed the backdoor gently behind him, before running upstairs to Gretel.

"Now we have nothing to be afraid of," he told her, showing her some of the pebbles. "But don't say a word about them when we set off tomorrow for the forest."

Early the next morning, so early that the sun was not yet up, Hansel and Gretel heard their stepmother's harsh voice telling them to hurry and get dressed. "We're taking you into the forest, today," she shouted. "So don't play about but get ready quickly."

There was nothing but stale crusts to eat for breakfast so the meal was quickly over. Then their stepmother gave Hansel and Gretel a slice of stale bread. "Don't eat it now. Keep it for your dinner," she warned them. "There will be nothing else."

As they set out, Hansel lingered behind, fingering the pebbles in his pocket and hoping that he could drop them, one by one, without being seen.

"Why do you walk so slowly?" his father called over his shoulder after they had gone some way into the forest.

"I keep turning round to see if I can catch sight of my little white cat on the roof," Hansel told him.

"What a fool you are!" snapped his stepmother. "Your white cat is more likely to be busy catching mice. Hurry up, if you don't want a slap."

When they reached the middle of the forest where the trees grew so close together that they blotted out the sun, their father told them to rest. "Your mother and I will gather as many sticks as we can," he said, giving Gretel a sad look. "But first I will make a fire for you while we are away so that you won't be cold."

Hansel and Gretel sat close together beside the fire, hoping against hope that their father would return. For a time they could hear the sound of his axe as he struck the trees. Then a silence fell upon the forest; even the little birds no longer sang.

"How dark it grows," said Gretel at last. "Oh, how frightened I am! They are not coming back for us, I am sure of it now."

Hansel put his arm round his sister's shoulder, as he said, "It is too dark now to follow my trail of pebbles. Let's try and get some sleep. Don't be afraid, Gretel. I'll take care of you."

Gretel closed her eyes, snuggling up close to her brother, and Hansel kept watch until at last the dark night sky was lit by the silvery light from the moon. "Come," he whispered softly to his sister, "it's time to go. I shall be able to find the pebbles easily now with the help of the friendly moon."

Hand in hand, the children set out and Hansel pointed out the pebbles as they walked along. "If we hurry," he said, "we shall be home by morning."

By early morning, Hansel and Gretel reached their cottage and oh, how happy they were to see their father again. And how happy he was too. He hugged and kissed them and vowed that never again would they be parted.

But his wife was not at all pleased to see the children. She scowled and turned away from them and the poor woodcutter knew it would not be long before she tried once again to lose them in the forest. How right he was!

One night, just a few days after their return, his wife said, "Nothing has changed. There is not enough food in the cupboard to feed a sparrow. We must take them into the forest early tomorrow morning and this time make certain that they do not find their way home."

Once again, the woodcutter pleaded and argued and once again the wife began to shout. And, as soon as the house was quiet, Hansel stole down the stairs.

"I will fill my pockets with shining white pebbles once more," he

told himself, as he reached the back door. "Then we will be saved again."

Alas, when Hansel tried to open the back door, he found it locked and the key missing. What could he do now? Safely back in bed, he thought and thought. At last, he made up his mind to use the bread his stepmother was sure to give him. "I'll lay a trail of breadcrumbs," he finally decided, before his eyes closed in sleep. "The crumbs will be just as good as the pebbles."

But, oh dear me, how wrong Hansel was! The next morning as they trudged further and further into the forest, Hansel dropped his crumbs. Can you guess what happened? All the little birds of the forest flew down from the trees and feasted on the bread!

Gretel began to cry bitterly when, once again, they found themselves all alone in the deep dark forest. "Don't cry, little sister," said Hansel. "My trail of breadcrumbs will help us to find our way home."

But as the moon lit the forest he discovered the awful truth. Not a single crumb could he find. But he was so brave that he smiled and whistled and pretended that he knew the way home even without the help of the breadcrumbs.

"I – I d–don't think we shall ever find our way h–home," Gretel sobbed, as Hansel took her hand. "We'll be eaten by wolves."

"It's too dark now to find the right path," Hansel told her. "Let's sleep a little as we did before and then start out. You're safe with me so don't cry."

Have you ever been lost in a big forest? Have you ever run along paths that lead nowhere and fallen into ditches and tripped over trailing branches? Have you ever been so frightened that you couldn't make your tired legs carry you another step?

It was just like that with Gretel after walking and running and walking again for nearly a whole day. She was so scared that at last she sat down and said she couldn't take another step. Hansel was tired and frightened too but being a boy he couldn't let his sister see his despair. "We must keep walking," he said at last. "We're sure to find the right path soon."

As he spoke, he suddenly saw on the branch of a tree just ahead of them a most beautiful white bird. It was like no other bird he had ever seen and he pointed to it. Gretel dried her eyes and stared at the bird.

"How pretty it is," she said. "Like a white dove but nicer." As she got up and ran towards it the bird flew to another tree a short distance away and once again perched motionless on a branch.

"It's just as if the bird wanted us to follow it," said Hansel. "Shall we, Gretel? Perhaps it will take us safely out of the forest."

Hand in hand, the children ran after the pretty white bird and soon they found themselves in a clearing in the forest and staring at the strangest little cottage you could ever imagine. The snow-white bird flew down and sat on the roof while Hansel and Gretel walked towards the cottage.

"Look!" Gretel cried, clapping her hands, "the walls are made of bread and covered with cakes."

"And the windows are made of clear sugar," exclaimed Hansel. "And the roof has tiles made of biscuits!"

"Oh, I'm so hungry," whispered Gretel. "Do – do you think we could have a tiny nibble?"

For answer, Hansel reached up and broke off a piece of roof and then Gretel began to eat some of the window. "It tastes just like barley sugar," she laughed. "I don't feel frightened any more."

Hansel had eaten quite a big part of the roof when suddenly the door opened, and a woman, all bent and wrinkled and old as old can be, hobbled out of the cottage on two crutches. At the sight of her, Gretel screamed and dropped her sugar windowpane, and Hansel said, "Begging your pardon, ma'am, we meant no harm."

The old woman smiled and nodded. "How glad I am to see you, dear children," she said, in a croaky kind of voice. "Do come in and stay with me. I will take care of you." And she took them both by the hand and led them inside.

"She looks like a witch," Gretel whispered to her brother, "but she can't be, she is so kind. Just look what she is giving us to eat."

The old woman busied herself setting out pancakes and honey on the table. And this was followed by sugared buns and apples and nuts.

"Eat all you can," she said, as she hobbled back and forward between the kitchen and the front room. "And drink your milk. Milk helps you to grow big and strong."

What a feast the children had and, afterwards, the old woman took them into another room and showed them two little beds covered with flowery sheets.

"There is where you will sleep," she croaked. "And in the morning I will show you some toys you can play with."

Now the old woman was really and truly a wicked witch. Her snow-white bird was trained to fly out into the forest and search for lost children and bring them to her. And whenever children fell into her power she fed them up to make them round and fat and then roasted them in her big oven.

If Hansel and Gretel had known anything about witches they would have looked at her red eyes and known her for what she was. But of course they had never before met a witch so they did not know.

Early the next morning, however, they learnt the truth. As soon as they were dressed, the witch seized Hansel and carried him outside.

"In you go," she cackled, thrusting him into a big cage. "When you are nice and plump I will eat you for my dinner."

Then she went back to Gretel. "Fetch the water from the well," she commanded. "Move yourself, you lazy child. From now on you will be my servant. And when I have eaten your brother I will fatten you up and eat you."

Of course poor Gretel burst into tears and begged for her brother's life but the wicked witch only laughed and drove her out of the house, telling her to make haste and fetch the water.

For the next few days the witch busied herself with her cooking. Apple pies smothered in cream were taken out to Hansel every hour and often there was chicken and baked potatoes and jam doughnuts. But for Gretel there was nothing but stale crusts of bread and cups of water to drink.

At the end of a week, the witch went to Hansel's cage and cried, "Hansel, Hansel, stretch out your finger so that I may feel if you grow fat!"

You may well wonder why the witch had to feel Hansel's finger but the truth is that witches cannot see very well.

Now Hansel was not only brave but clever. Instead of giving the witch his finger to feel, he thrust out a chicken bone.

"I cannot understand it," the witch grumbled after two weeks. "You eat everything I give you yet you grow no fatter." And so angry was she that she pushed Gretel into a corner of the kitchen and refused even to feed her on scraps.

At the end of a month the witch vowed she would wait no longer. "I will eat that brother of yours today," she cried. "Be he fat or thin he will be baked in my oven." And she told Gretel to fetch water while she lit the oven.

When Gretel returned, the witch said, "I have lit the oven but I cannot tell whether or not it is hot enough. Creep inside and see if it is properly heated."

But Gretel guessed that she meant to trap her in the oven and bake her first, so she said, "I – I do not know how to get in. Won't you show me?"

"What a stupid girl you are!" exclaimed the witch, impatiently. "The door is big enough. Watch me! I'll show you." And she opened the heavy door and put her head inside the oven.

Gretel knew what she must do. Suddenly brave, she crept up behind the witch and with a great push, sent her toppling into the oven. Then she slammed shut the heavy door. And that was the end of the terrible witch for there was no way out of the oven and she had no powers that would save her from being baked.

With a shout of joy, Gretel ran outside to the cage where her brother was a prisoner and set him free. Then together they ran back to the house. "I have seen where she keeps her treasure," said Gretel. "She has boxes filled with pearls and rubies and diamonds. Do you think we could take some back to our father?"

"Witches' treasure belongs to the one who finds it," said Hansel wisely. "So let us help ourselves."

Then Gretel showed him where the witch had hidden her treasure under the floorboards and Hansel filled his pockets with precious stones and then Gretel filled the pockets of her little apron. When they could carry no more, they ran out into the forest.

After walking for at least two hours, they came at last to a stretch of water. "What shall we do now?" Gretel asked. "Hansel, what shall we do? We cannot swim across this water and there is no boat."

Hansel sat down to think and Gretel looked all about her. Presently a white duck came swimming over the water and she cried,

"Little duck, little duck, can you see,
　Hansel and Gretel waiting for you?
　There's not a boat, or a bridge in sight,
　Take us across on your back so white."

To her joy, the duck swam over to them and Hansel sprang to his feet. "Do you think she will take us?" he asked.

"I know she will," said Gretel happily. "But we shall be too heavy for her if we both ride on her back. I will go first and then tell her to return for you."

So the good little duck carried first Gretel and then Hansel across the broad lake and when they were safely on the other side, Hansel said he was sure he could find his way home from there.

Soon they came upon the path which led them straight to their father's house and, in a few moments, they saw it among the trees. Gretel began to run and Hansel followed her, shouting with joy. As they burst into the kitchen, their father looked up from the table where he so often sat with his head in his hands, thinking about his long-lost children.

At first, he thought it was a dream but Gretel's warm arms were soon about his neck and Hansel was emptying his pockets on the table to show him the rubies and diamonds and pearls that would make them rich.

"Your stepmother is dead," the woodcutter said, at last. "And I am all alone. Day after day I have spent in sadness thinking that you were both lost to me for ever."

Then Hansel told his father the whole story, from beginning to end, and the woodcutter said, "I care nothing for the precious stones. All I care about is that I have my beloved children safely back home. Now we shall be happy for always."

And they were, too. And there was always bread and meat in the cupboard for, after the woodcutter had sold the precious stones, there was enough money to buy everything they needed for the rest of their lives.

The Snow Man

ONCE UPON a time there was a Snow Man who was quite certain he was going to live for ever. He was born around Christmas in the yard close to a kennel where the housekeeper's dog lived. He had two pieces of slate instead of eyes and his mouth was made out of an old rake which meant his teeth were strong enough to hold a clay pipe.

"It's a shame I can't move," he remarked to the bulldog, as together they watched the moon rise in the dark sky. "You can see for yourself how big and strong I am. I could do great things if only I could get about."

"The sun will soon make you go," snapped the old dog, who had little respect for Snow Men. "I saw it happen last year with one of your kind, and the year before, too."

"I don't believe it," said the Snow Man. "I simply don't believe it. When I move, it will be because I want to and not because the sun tells me to."

"You wait and see," retorted the bulldog. "You may not have so long to wait either, for there's a twitching in my legs that tells me the weather is going to change. That cold wind you seem to enjoy so much is going to disappear."

The weather did change but it was still much to the Snow Man's liking. The wind was icy now and his whole body crackled with pleasure. It is true the sun came out and stared at him, but, though the trees began to sparkle just as if diamond dust had been scattered over them, the sun made no impression on the Snow Man.

"The sun can't do anything to me," boasted the Snow Man, as the bitter wind blew all round him. "I told you, didn't I?"

"Wait," grunted the bulldog wisely. "Just you wait!"

Presently a boy and a girl came into the yard and stood looking at the Snow Man. "Isn't he fine and fat?" laughed the girl, and the boy put his arm round her waist.

"We made a good job of him this year," said the boy. "I hope he lasts . . ."

"So do I," thought the Snow Man. "So do I." And he waited anxiously for the girl's reply. But she only laughed merrily and danced up and down making the hard snow crackle under her feet. Then she ran away and the boy chased after her.

"Are they the same kind of beings as you and I?" asked the Snow Man, watching them go.

"Well, they belong to the same master," answered the dog. "People like you, born only a day or two ago, can't hope to know anything. Now I know everything and everyone in the house. There was a time when I did not lie here in the cold, fastened to a chain."

"The cold is wonderful," said the Snow Man. "But tell me how it happened that you left the house."

"To begin with," answered the bulldog, clanking his chain, "I lay in a chair covered with soft velvet and my master and mistress made a great fuss of me, kissing my nose and wiping my paws whenever I got them wet. But soon I grew too big to sit on their laps and they lost interest in me. Then the housekeeper adopted me."

"I don't suppose you minded too much," said the Snow Man. "I don't suppose you enjoyed the kissing . . ."

"Not much," admitted the bulldog. "And certainly the housekeeper had a most comfortable room in the basement and the food was just as good as it was upstairs. I had my own cushion and more time to myself. And, of course, there was the stove. I slept under the stove in the winter; it was the best time of the whole year then . . ."

"Stove?" questioned the Snow Man. "What is stove?"

"The most beautiful thing in the house," said the dog with feeling. "Do you know I still dream of that stove . . ."

"Was it – was she white like me?" asked the Snow Man, interested. "Did she – er – look like me in any way?"

"Not in the least," said the dog. "The stove is as black as a crow, with a long neck and four legs. It eats firewood and the fire comes out of its mouth but there is nothing to be afraid of if you keep to the side or go underneath."

"Is she – it – still there?" asked the Snow Man, now greatly interested.

"Certainly," said the bulldog. "You can see the stove through the basement from where you stand."

The Snow Man looked and saw the bright, polished stove with the fire gleaming from its lower half. And the strangest feeling came over him. It was as if he had known the stove for a very long time and she was calling to him to come to her.

"Why ever did you leave her?" demanded the Snow Man, when his senses returned and he felt able to speak. "How could you leave her?"

"It was all a matter of temper," grunted the bulldog. "I lost my temper one morning with the housekeeper's youngest nephew. He tried to take my bone and I just couldn't allow that. In fact, I snapped – well, perhaps it was more than a snap, a nibble of his left leg, just the smallest bite, you understand. But the housekeeper was angry. She brought me out here that same morning and chained me up in the kennel. That happened years ago, when I was quite young, but house-keepers have long memories, you understand."

"I understand," said the Snow Man, "and I'm sorry." But he no longer seemed interested. His eyes were once again fixed on the stove on its four delicate legs. "She's just about my size," he murmured tenderly. "Not much taller!"

"What did you say?" asked the bulldog.

"Nothing of importance," answered the Snow Man. "It's just that I have a strange strong feeling for the stove. I feel so drawn to her that I long to be with her."

"If you do get near her," warned the dog, "you will melt away, right away."

"I don't care," replied the Snow Man, "I feel myself breaking up as it is."

For the whole of that day the Snow Man stood looking in through the basement window and, when darkness fell, he saw the stove begin to glow in the dark room almost as if she were beckoning to him. That night it was so cold that the Snow Man crackled and crackled and he thought, "I'm not breaking up, after all. There's life in me yet. My chance to meet the stove may yet come."

In the morning the window-panes of the basement were all covered with ice and the stove was no longer visible. The Snow Man shivered. He no longer looked quite so fat and jolly and his friend remarked, "I know what's the matter with you, you're stove-sick. It's the kind of sickness that sometimes takes hold of humans, though they call it love-sick. But I must admit it's the first time I've known a Snow Man to fall in love with a stove. It's a puzzle. Anyway, the weather is going to change – it may not suit you at all."

The weather did change. It began to thaw and the more it thawed the thinner the Snow Man grew. "I'm getting smaller and smaller," he confessed to the dog. "It must be my stove-sickness."

"It's the weather," said the dog, knowingly. "I have seen it happen before. Tomorrow there will be nothing left of you."

The Snow Man made no reply for now he could see through the basement window again and his eyes were fixed on the stove, all black and shiny.

The next morning the Snow Man just crumbled away. The boy and girl ran out of the house to look at the heap of snow and to rescue the clay pipe for another year. "It's quite sad to see the end of our Snow Man," said the girl. "He was the best we ever made."

"It was my idea to build him round a pole," said the boy.

"Fixing the shovel to the pole helped him to stand up straight," said the girl, "and that was my idea. We must take the shovel back to the stove. That's where it belongs."

"Ah," thought the dog, as he lay listening. "Now I understand everything! That Snow Man had something of the stove's inside him. That explains his stove-sickness; it's all perfectly clear now."

And satisfied that he had solved the mystery, he forgot all about the Snow Man and went to sleep.

The Donkey Skin

ONCE UPON a time, there lived a King who had many wonderful possessions. But visitors who came to his palace to admire his paintings and gold and silver trinkets and furniture were always taken first to the stable to see a little brown donkey that stood in a fine stable inlaid with marble.

"I love my little donkey far more than I love my paintings or my gold," the King would say with a smile. "And I would rather spend my time talking to my donkey than looking at my priceless paintings and possessions."

Now although the King loved his donkey, he also greatly loved his beautiful wife and daughter and was extremely proud of them. His daughter grew up so much like her mother that sometimes it was difficult to tell the two apart.

One sad day, the Queen became desperately ill. The King sat all night by her bedside begging her to tell him that she would recover. But the Queen knew that she was soon going to die and when morning came, she whispered, "Promise me you will marry again and that you will choose a wife who is as wise and beautiful as I. This is my last wish."

The King, in deep distress, gave his promise and soon afterwards the Queen died. The death of his beloved Queen changed the King out of all recognition. He grew pale and thin, lost his appetite and no longer knew his servants. But worst of all, he no longer knew his daughter when she spoke to him.

As the months passed, the King began to think of himself as a young Prince again and whenever he met his daughter in the palace he mistook her for the girl he had once loved and wooed. He called her by her mother's name and begged her to be his wife.

Her father's strange madness so alarmed and upset the gentle Princess that, at last, she fled from the palace. "I will go to my godmother," she thought, as she took the road that led to the sea. "She is so wise and clever that she will surely be able to help me."

Now the Princess's godmother was the Fairy of the Lilac Tree. Her house was a pretty little grotto at the edge of the sea and she had decorated it with coral and mother-of-pearl. It was very beautiful and the whole place smelled sweetly of lilac.

"I know why you have come, Christabel," said the fairy, as soon as the Princess entered the grotto. "Your father, the King, has lost his reason and sees you as the girl he first loved long ago."

"That is true," said Christabel, unhappily. "He grows very angry when I tell him that I am really his daughter. Oh, what am I to do?"

"When next he asks you to be his wife you must ask him for something he will find very difficult to give you," said the fairy.

"My father is very rich," said the Princess. "He can give me anything."

"Ask him for a dress the colour of the sky," advised the fairy.

"I will," said the Princess, smiling faintly for the first time for many days. "Thank you, godmother."

So she returned to the palace and the very next day the King sent for her and asked her to be his wife.

"I cannot marry you, sire," said Christabel, "until you have given me a dress the colour of the sky."

The King nodded and that same day sent for his weavers and his tailors. In fear of their lives they worked, day and night, until, at last, they had made a dress that held all the beauty of a blue sky on a summer's day. And yet so cunningly woven was the material that when its wearer moved, it seemed that soft white clouds floated among the folds.

Satisfied, the King summoned his daughter. "Here is your dress,"

he said. "Is it not the colour of the sky?" And the Princess was forced to admit that the wonderful dress did exactly resemble the sky.

Disappointed and frightened, she ran from the palace, thinking that her godmother would hide her in the grotto.

"You cannot stay here, child," said the fairy. "Your father would soon discover you. No, you must return to him and ask him for a dress the colour of the moon. This time, I am sure, he will not be able to give it to you."

But the fairy was wrong. Once again, the King commanded his weavers and tailors, on pain of death, to make a dress the colour of the moon and in three days it was ready.

The dress was so skilfully embroidered that when the Princess saw it she was forced to say, "Yes, yes, this wonderful dress makes me think of the silvery moon on a clear night."

Once again, Christabel ran to her godmother to ask her what to do. "Ask him for a dress like the sun," said the fairy.

But, for the third time, the King granted Christabel's wish. So dazzling was the dress this time that the girl could scarcely look at it and yet, strangely, it made all who saw it think of golden sunshine, for it was afire with countless precious stones stitched to the skirt and bodice.

"He is too clever for us," Christabel told her godmother as she sat in despair in the grotto. "What can we do now?"

"You must ask for the skin of the brown donkey," her godmother said, after thinking for a long while. "The donkey is his most cherished possession; even in his madness, he loves his donkey, and will surely refuse to have it killed."

"How can you ask me to do such a thing?" protested the Princess. "It would break my father's heart if he were to lose his donkey."

"Go back to the palace," said her godmother sternly, "and do as I say. It is the only way."

The King was waiting for Christabel when she entered the palace. "I have given you a dress like the sky, a dress like the moon and a dress like the sun," he said. "I have carried out all your wishes. Now you must be my wife."

Poor Christabel! She began to tremble as she saw her father's wild eyes and angry look.

"There is only one more thing I want," she whispered. "I must have the brown donkey's skin."

The King turned away, shaking his head and Christabel thought,

"Now at last his madness will leave him . . ." But it was not to be. That same day her father had the donkey killed and the donkey-skin sent to the Princess.

Sobbing bitterly, Christabel took the donkey-skin to the godmother. "All is lost," she said. "I must leave the palace for ever."

"If you do," said the fairy, "you must wear the donkey-skin. "Your father will send his soldiers to search for you. You will be easily found if you do not disguise yourself. This donkey-skin will make you look so ugly that the soldiers will pass you by."

The Princess shuddered at the very idea of wearing the donkey-skin but she knew her godmother spoke truly. As long as she wore the donkey-skin she would be safe.

Then her godmother gave her a parting gift, a thin gold ring set with an emerald. "You have only to twist the ring," said the fairy, "and a chest, packed to the brim with some of your most beautiful dresses and jewellery, will appear. There will be moments when you wish to dress as a Princess and knowing that you can do so will give you courage to endure wearing the donkey-skin."

Christabel slipped the ring on to her finger, kissed her godmother affectionately and set off on foot down the long road that would take her out of her father's kingdom. For many days and nights she trudged along and sometimes a kind-hearted villager gave her food and sometimes a farmer allowed her to sleep in his barn.

When the Princess was safely across the border and in a country ruled over by another king, she stopped at a farmhouse to ask for work.

"I will do any kind of task you set me," she told the farmer's wife. "I do not care what it is."

"I dare say you will," said the woman sharply, "for a girl as plain as you will find it difficult to get work."

In her hideous donkey-skin, Christabel did indeed look ugly but she did not dare take it off. "Then I can stay?" she asked humbly. And the farmer's wife nodded. "You can stay," she said, "if you're willing to clean out the pigsty and do the scrubbing throughout the house."

Then Christabel was taken to a small dark room at the end of a long passage. "You can sleep here," said her new mistress.

Now the farm where Christabel found herself was no ordinary farm; it belonged to a Prince who often visited it when out hunting. He kept many beautiful birds at the farm and it was his delight to come and feed them. Whenever the Prince was due for another visit the farm was scrubbed and cleaned and the servants warned that they must be on their best behaviour.

Christabel soon learnt about the Prince's visits but she was kept so busy cleaning and scrubbing that only once did she catch a glimpse of him. Sometimes, however, on a Sunday morning when the family and the servants had all gone to Church, Christabel found time to visit the aviary and look at the Prince's beautiful birds. "If only I could show others how I really look," she would think as she stood listening to their sweet singing.

One Sunday morning, greatly daring, Christabel twisted the slender gold ring her godmother had given her and wished that she might once again dress up as a Princess. Almost before she could turn round, there on her little bed, sat the chest filled to the top with wonderful dresses. With a cry of happiness, she chose the most beautiful and casting aside her ugly donkey-skin, slipped into it. Oh, how good it was to look herself again and for a few minutes the Princess forgot all her unhappiness as she sat before her cracked mirror, combing out her long golden hair.

When the other servants returned, they found "Donkey-skin"

as they unkindly called her, scrubbing the great copper pans and, as usual, they teased her and sent her about their errands as well as hers.

Now one Sunday the Prince himself came unannounced to the farmhouse. Who knows what mysterious part the Fairy of the Lilac Tree might have had to do with this visit! But when the Prince could find no one in the farm to welcome him, he wandered down the long narrow passage and came upon the tiny room where Christabel spent her happy, solitary Sunday mornings. The door was shut and locked but the Prince could hear someone singing so softly and sweetly that it reminded him of his precious birds. Filled with curiosity, he knelt down and peeped through the keyhole and there he saw not an ugly servant girl, but a glorious Princess in a dress of silvery blue, with diamonds in her hair. So beautiful was the sight, that the Prince could scarcely tear himself away.

But after all he was a Prince! "I will not tell her how I first saw her," he decided. "I will return tomorrow and ask the farmer's wife to introduce us in a proper manner."

Early the next morning the Prince rode out to the farm. "You have a beautiful young girl staying with you," he said to the farmer's wife, who rushed out to greet him. "Will you bring her to me?"

"A beautiful girl!" the woman repeated mystified. "There is no one here, sire, as you must know, except the servant girls, and you have seen most of them except perhaps old Donkey-skin and she is certainly no beauty!"

The Prince was so certain that the farmer's wife was mistaken that he questioned several of the serving girls. "Tell me," he said, "where is the golden-haired girl who lives here? What kind of work does she do about the farm?"

The girls looked at him in amazement, assuring him that there was no girl with golden-hair among them. "We should know," said one of the servants with a toss of her head. "We are all here, except Donkey-skin, and she is as plain as a pikestaff."

Troubled in mind and deeply unhappy, the Prince returned to the palace. So upset was he that by the end of the week he had fallen into a fever, and was quite unable to eat and sleep. His mother, the Queen, was so worried she sent for the royal doctor.

"You must try and carry out his every wish," the old doctor told the Queen. "No matter what he asks for, see that he has it. In time the fever may pass but first his mind must be at peace."

One night, as the Queen sat by her son's bedside, she heard him murmur Donkey-skin's name. "She must bake me a cake with her own hands," the Prince whispered. "Tell her."

Now the Queen had never heard of Donkey-skin but in the morning she soon learnt where the girl worked, and she sent a royal messenger to the farm with her son's request.

"Gracious me!" exclaimed the farmer's wife. "The young Prince must be out of his mind to be thinking of Donkey-skin. She is the plainest and poorest of our servants."

"Nevertheless the Queen commands it," said the messenger. "I will return this afternoon for the cake."

"And you shall have it," said the farmer's wife, and she sent for Donkey-skin. "Wash your hands and put on this big white apron," she told the girl. "Today, you must bake a cake that is fit for a King's son to eat."

Then she gave Donkey-skin flour and eggs and butter and sugar and left her alone in the kitchen. As Christabel made the batter,

the ring which her fairy godmother had given her, slipped from her finger into the batter. Now, some say that the Princess dropped her ring on purpose into the cake but others are equally certain that it was just an accident.

The cake was taken to the palace and as he bit into it the Prince came upon the thin gold band. That same day, when his mother came to see him, he vowed that he would marry the girl who could wear the ring.

Surprised and alarmed at her son's words, the Queen decided that her son's fever had increased. She pleaded with him but the Prince obstinately refused to listen to everything she said to make him change his mind. "Find me the girl who can wear this tiny ring," he insisted, over and over again.

At last the Queen left the room to seek advice again from her royal physician. "Do as he says," decided the old man. "He will not recover from this fever unless you do."

So then the Queen summoned all the princesses and high-born ladies to the palace to try the ring. Many had long, slim delicate fingers but always the ring was too small. So anxious were some of the ladies to succeed that they rubbed their fingers with turnips in an effort to make them thinner! But it was to no avail. The ring fitted none of them.

After the noble ladies came the needle-women and the spinsters, many of whom also had beautiful hands. But they, too, failed to pass the test. Then came the servant girls with their red rough hands and, oh, how they giggled and jostled each other as they tried in vain to push the ring on to their thick fingers.

When the Queen was satisfied that she had done everything possible to carry out her son's request, she hurried to his bedside. "There is not a girl in the land who can wear the ring," she told him. "I give you my word that all have tried."

"Have you asked Donkey-skin?" the Prince asked.

"No," admitted the Queen. "All the other girls from the farm have tried the ring but Donkey-skin was not among them. I suppose her mistress considered her too plain and ugly to send her to the palace."

"She must be allowed to try," insisted the Prince. "I found the ring in her cake. Let Donkey-skin be brought to the palace.

So the Queen sent her royal messenger to the farm to fetch Donkey-skin. When Christabel saw her ring again, she smiled happily. "The

ring is mine," she told the lady-in-waiting, who held it out to her. "See how it fits my finger!"

"I must take you to the Queen," said the lady-in-waiting, scarcely able to believe her own eyes. "And what she will say I dare not think for the girl who can wear this ring is promised to her son."

"Let me return to the farm first," Christabel pleaded. "I must do what I can to make myself tidy."

No sooner was Christabel alone in her tiny room than she twisted her magic ring and instantly the chest appeared. From it she chose the shimmering moon dress that, long ago, her father had given her, and put it on. Then she covered it completely with the hideous donkey-skin.

The Prince himself was waiting for her when she entered the palace. He spoke to her kindly, doing his best to hide his disappointment as he looked at her. "I will keep my promise to wed you," he said gently. "There is no doubt that the ring belongs to you."

As he spoke, Christabel threw off the donkey-skin to show him a girl so radiantly beautiful that the Prince dropped to one knee in front of her. "You are the girl I saw at the farm!" he cried. "The only girl in the world for me!"

As the Prince kissed her hand the sweet scent of lilac filled the room and the Fairy of the Lilac Tree appeared. "I have come," she said, "to tell you Donkey-skin's story. There is nothing to spoil her happiness or yours for she is a true Princess."

So, amid great rejoicing, the Prince and the Princess were married and chief among the guests was Christabel's own father, now cured of his madness and able to rejoice in his daughter's happiness.

The Fisherman and his Wife

ONCE UPON a time a fisherman lived with his wife in a miserable hut close to the sea. Of all the fishermen who fished the seas, this fisherman was the most unlucky. From early morning to late at night, he fished and fished and fished, but he never caught anything.

Then one day his luck changed. He cast his line overboard and, almost immediately, he felt a tug. When he pulled it in towards him, caught on the hook, was a big Flounder.

The poor fisherman could have wept for joy at this unexpected bit of luck. But just as he was about to pull the fish into his boat, it began speaking to him.

"Don't kill me," said the Flounder. "Let me live. Besides it will do you no good if you do kill me. I shall certainly not be at all nice to eat for I am an enchanted prince and will not taste like a fish."

"Bless my soul!" exclaimed the astonished fisherman. "A talking fish! Now what would I do with such a fish – a talking fish that says he is a prince? No, I couldn't bring myself to take your life. I'll have to set you free – go back into the sea."

That night when he returned home empty-handed, as usual, the fisherman tried to stop his wife's angry words by describing the talking fish. "He did say he was an enchanted prince," he ended his story.

"A Prince, did you say?" questioned his wife. "Have you no sense, husband? You should have asked him a favour. Did you tell him about our miserable hut here that is no better than a pigsty? Surely he could have done something about that."

The fisherman shook his head and his wife went on. "You must return to the same spot tomorrow. If you're lucky enough to catch that talking fish again, tell him you want a favour from him before you drop him back into the sea."

Now the fisherman was a good man who was content with very little. His wife, however, was quite different. She was greedy and quick-tempered, but the fisherman was afraid of her. "Very well, Isobel," he said. "I will get the boat out early tomorrow morning."

The sea was stormy and dark and threatening when the fisherman set out the next day. When he arrived at the spot where he had caught the Flounder, he thought that he had little chance of catching it a second time. So he stood up in his boat, that rocked violently on the waves, and called out:

"Flounder, Flounder in the sea,
Come, I pray thee, here to me.
Remember, once I set thee free."

To his great relief, the fisherman almost at once saw the Flounder swim up to his boat. "What do you want?" the fish asked.

"It's not me, you understand," said the fisherman. "It's my wife, Isobel. She says that I ought to have asked for a favour from you before I let you go yesterday. You see, we live in a miserable hut, which is really little better than a pigsty. She would like to have something better – a cottage, perhaps?"

"Go back home," said the Flounder. "She has it already."

When the fisherman returned home he found his wife sitting on a bench in front of a small, neat cottage. She smiled when she saw him and led him inside. "Just look!" she cried. "We have a proper bedroom and a sitting-room and it is all so pretty and nicely furnished. I declare I am delighted with our good fortune."

Then she took her husband's hand and pulled him towards the backdoor. There, outside in the yard, were six fat hens and a shed filled with grain.

"Isn't it splendid?" exclaimed his wife. "I really am quite content. I will never ask for anything more."

The fisherman went out fishing every day just as usual but now there was no need to worry if he returned empty-handed for the hens always laid plenty of eggs and these his wife could sell in the market.

After two or three weeks of life in their new cottage, Isobel said to him one night as they sat by the window, "I don't know how you feel, husband, but today when I dusted our sitting-room I thought how small it was. As for the kitchen, I can scarcely turn round in it. It's quite impossibly tiny."

"I am very happy here," said the fisherman. "This cottage is like a palace compared with our old pigsty."

"The cottage may be good enough for you," snapped his wife. "But it seems to me we could have done much better for ourselves. Instead of asking for a simple cottage we should have asked for a castle. Just imagine what life would be like in a big stone castle! I would be a grand lady and you could live like a lord!"

Her husband shook his head. "I don't like it, Isobel," he said at last. "I know what you are trying to make me do. You want me to go back to the Flounder and ask him to give us a castle."

71

"Indeed I do!" exclaimed his wife. "And there will be no hot meals for you in this house until you do!"

The fisherman did his best to reason with his wife, but he was too quiet and gentle to stand up to her for long. So that same week he rowed out to the spot where he had last spoken to the Flounder. The sea looked purple and angry as he stood up in his boat and called:

"Flounder, Flounder in the sea,
Come, I pray thee, here to me.
Remember, once I set thee free."

"Well, what do you want now?" asked the Flounder, appearing immediately.

"It's not for myself that I ask," said the old man in a humble voice. "It's for my good wife, Isobel. She wants to live in a big stone castle."

"Go back," said the Flounder. "You'll find her standing on the steps of such a castle."

The fisherman rowed back to the shore and there, instead of the little white-washed cottage, stood a great stone castle. His wife waved to him from the big, stone steps as he pulled his boat up on to the beach. "I can scarcely wait to show you round," she cried impatiently, as he came towards her. "This is a magnificent place. You should see the chairs and tables. They're made of gold and there are paintings on the walls that must have cost a fortune. As for the cellars – there are bottles of wine and all kinds of other drink that I don't even know the name of. . . ."

In her excitement, Isobel took hold of her husband's arm and pulled him up the steps and into the vast hall of the castle. The old man rubbed his eyes as he saw all the gold and silver and the rich carpets.

"But you haven't seen half of it yet!" cried his wife. "Come out into the courtyard. It's big enough to hold a dozen cottages. There are fine horses in the stables and grooms to look after them and behind the courtyard there's a garden that would do credit to a palace."

The fisherman said very little as he walked round the castle. And when at last he sat down to eat he could scarcely bring himself to speak at all to the servants who appeared with delicious food on plates of gold. But his wife was enjoying every minute of it and she spoke to the servants as if she was used to being waited on.

When they were alone, the fisherman turned to his wife and said, "Let us be content this time, Isobel. We have come a long way from our pigsty. Do not, I beg you, ask for anything grander than this."

"We shall see," said his wife with a sly smile. "We shall see."

The next morning, instead of going out to sea, the fisherman walked alone in the beautiful garden, admiring the flowers and listening to the birds singing. "Surely," he thought, "surely, she will ask for nothing more. What more could she want?"

But alas, the fisherman's greedy wife was still not satisfied. The castle filled with gold and silver and wonderful paintings was certainly very grand. But supposing, just supposing, it could be changed into a palace. "Then I would be the King," Isobel thought. "Kings live in palaces. My husband wouldn't want to be King. I would be King . . ."

"Husband," she cried, as soon as the fisherman came in from the garden. "I want to be King. Oh, I know that fish of yours has done quite well so far. But if he can give us a castle then he can give us a palace. And if I have a palace I shall be King. I want to be King."

In vain, her husband tried to make her change her mind. But she gave him no peace at all, and kept repeating over and over again, "I want to be King, I want to be King," until at last the poor man rushed out of the castle and down to the beach.

Slowly he pushed his boat out to sea and rowed out to the place where he knew the great fish to be. This time the sea was an angry grey and the water all around him had a strange horrid smell that reminded him of rotting seaweed. The fisherman trembled with fear and his voice was low as he mumbled,

> *"Flounder, Flounder in the sea,*
> *Come, I pray thee, here to me.*
> *Remember, once I set thee free."*

The Flounder appeared at once. "What do you want now?" he asked.

"My good wife, Isobel, wants to be King," he whispered. "She wants a palace and a crown."

"Go home," said the Flounder. "She is King already."

Scarcely knowing what to expect, the fisherman rowed slowly

homewards. Long before he reached the shore, he saw the castle, glistening in the sunshine. Sentries stood at its gates and soldiers with trumpets marched up and down, up and down, in the square before the palace.

The fisherman saw no sign of his wife as he entered the palace. His eyes took in the carved chairs, the tapestries of brilliant colours that hung upon the walls, the columns of marble that shone in the sunlight. Servants rushed hither and thither brushing him aside in their haste and the fisherman almost fled.

"If you are looking for the King," a young man in splendid red velvet said to him, "you will find His Majesty in the Throne Room at the end of the hall."

The fisherman walked softly, almost on tiptoe, as he entered the Throne Room and there, on a golden throne, sat his wife. She wore a crown of diamonds and rubies on her head and her fingers sparkled with rings.

Around the throne stood twelve ladies-in-waiting who bowed respectfully as the fisherman approached the throne. "Well, wife," he said. "You are King. Now you are the ruler of the land. Are you content yet?"

"Yes, I am King," said his wife. "And I have a palace any King would be proud to own. But it is still not enough. After all, there is one greater than I."

The fisherman covered his ears but he could not shut out his wife's voice as she shouted, "I want to be Emperor. Go back and tell the Flounder to make me Emperor. It is the least he can do."

At first the fisherman stubbornly refused to return to the sea. But when his wife told him she would have his head cut off as a warning to others who might dare to disobey her, he gave in meekly once more.

This time the sea was an inky black when he called out to the great fish:

> *"Flounder, Flounder in the sea,*
> *Come, I pray thee, here to me,*
> *Remember, once I set thee free."*

"Well, what is it this time?" asked the Flounder, as he rose out of the sea.

"It's my good wife, Isobel," answered the fisherman in a voice full of shame. "You have made her King. Now, she wants to be Emperor."

"Go," said the Flounder. "You will find that she is Emperor already."

The fisherman rowed himself back to the shore. There stood a palace, twice as magnificent as the one he had left just a short time ago. Its gold walls glistened and shimmered in the sunshine, almost as if they were on fire. The fisherman blinked and turned away. All around him were marching soldiers in splendid uniforms.

With his head bowed, the fisherman went into the palace to search for his wife. He found her, at last, seated on a throne of solid gold.

Soldiers blew silver trumpets as he walked towards her. He saw that on her head was a crown, as high as a young tree and glittering with diamonds and emeralds as big as eggs.

"Wife," said he, as he drew near to the throne, "are you now the Emperor?"

"Yes," she replied, slowly and grandly, "I am the Emperor!"

"Then be content," he said. "Ask for nothing more from the Flounder."

"Why do you stand there like a fool?" cried his wife. "I am the Emperor but I cannot hold back the sea or make the sun rise and set. Go back to the Flounder and tell him that I wish to be equal to God."

The poor fisherman felt himself grow faint with horror. He shuddered and began to sway on his feet. But his wife showed him no mercy. She worked herself up into such a rage that the soldiers flung themselves face downwards on the marble floor in terror.

"The Flounder cannot do that," her husband managed to whisper at last. "He can make you King and Emperor but he cannot make you equal to God."

"Go!" shrieked his wife, the tall crown swaying as she rose, a terrifying figure, to her feet. "Go, go, go!"

The fisherman ran like a madman from the palace down to the sea. As he pushed out his boat, the thunder rolled and lightning flashed. The towering waves were black, flecked with grey and when the fisherman cried out to the great fish he could scarcely hear his own voice.

"Flounder, Flounder in the sea,
Come, I pray thee, here to me.
Remember, once I set thee free."

Lightning streaked the inky black sky with brilliant flashes as the Flounder came out of the sea. "Well," he said, "what is it now?"

"She – she – she wants to be God," whispered the fisherman, trembling in every limb.

"Go!" said the Flounder. "You will find her in the pigsty that was once her home."

The fisherman almost wished that the towering waves would

swallow him up as he rowed back to the shore. As he dragged his boat on to the sand he saw that the wonderful golden palace had vanished. How empty the place seemed. No marching soldiers; no processions of richly dressed lords and ladies! Instead, there was only the broken-down hut, the pigsty, where he and Isobel had spent so much of their lives.

Then he saw her. She was the Isobel he remembered best of all. She wore the same long patched dress that she had worn when first he knew her. It reached down to her broken slippers and made her look tall. But, oh, how grey and lined her face was! And her hair – why it was twisted in the same ugly knot on top of her head that he had come

to dislike over the years. "She had everything for a while, but she lost everything through her greed," thought the fisherman sadly, as he went towards her.

Many times in the years that followed the fisherman cast his line into the sea. But though he fished and fished, from early morning to late at night, never again did he catch sight of the Flounder, and never again did he speak of the great fish to his wife. But sometimes, as they sat together, huddled over a miserable fire, Isobel would say, "Yes, yes, once I was Emperor and ruled the whole world."

The Little Mermaid

ONCE UPON a time there was a beautiful little mermaid. Her father was the Sea King and she lived with him and her five sisters in a wonderful palace in the deepest part of the ocean.

The Sea King's daughters were all very pretty but the prettiest of all was the youngest, the little mermaid, whose skin was as fresh as rose petals and whose eyes were as blue as cornflowers.

The little mermaid was quieter than her sisters. Her playthings were the fishes with gold and silver scales that swam all day in and out of the castle. She did not enjoy visiting the shipwrecks as her sisters did and she was sad whenever a poor broken ship sank to the bottom of the sea. Whenever this happened she hid in the beautiful gardens that surrounded her father's castle. Here, among the red and dark blue flowers and the golden fruits, she dreamt of the moment she was longing for – the moment when she would be fifteen years old.

The reason that she longed for this time was that on her fifteenth birthday, every sea maiden was allowed to swim wherever she pleased. If she wanted to, she could rise to the surface of the sea and sit on the rocks or swim close to the shore where the earth people lived. Once, the little mermaid had found a boy statue with a gentle, handsome face that had come from a shipwreck. She had carefully carried the boy statue back with her to her own special part of the garden and it had become her dearest possession. It was because of the statue that she longed so much to see the earth people for herself.

At last the day came when the Sea King's youngest daughter was fifteen years old. Her wise old grandmother had told her much about the earth people, and now she would be able to see them for herself.

"You will find them strange," her grandmother told her, as they sat together on her birthday. "Our bodies end in graceful fishes' tails. They walk on two supports that are called legs."

"Then we can never be truly like them?" asked the mermaid.

"No," said her grandmother. "We cannot shed tears like the earth people and we do not look forward to another life above the heavens as they do. When we die we become foam on the waves of the sea. But we live much longer than they do – for three hundred years, and we have much to make us happy."

"I long to know the earth people," murmured the mermaid, but her grandmother pretended not to hear.

"You are the loveliest of the Sea King's daughters," the wise old mermaid went on. "And you have the most beautiful singing voice of all the sea maidens. You should be very happy."

Then her grandmother placed a garland of white flowers that were really priceless pearls on the Princess's golden hair, and on her long glistening tail she fastened eight large oysters.

"They hurt!" protested the mermaid.

"That does not matter," said her grandmother sternly. "The oysters are a sign of your rank. Those you meet on your travels will know that you are a daughter of a King when they see the oysters."

When she was quite ready, the Princess said goodbye to her family and her friends. Then she rose like a water-bubble up through the blue

sea. As she lifted her head above the waves, she could see the bright stars and the pale crimson of the sky. But more beautiful than the stars and sky was the great ship with three masts that rocked gently at its anchor nearby. The little mermaid had never before seen such a ship nor the sailors who sailed her.

There was music coming from the ship and as the night grew darker, hundreds of lanterns were lit and men and women, beautifully and richly dressed, crowded the deck. Presently the mermaid saw a young man appear, laughing merrily and holding a glass in his hand. Oh, how handsome he was and how he reminded her of the boy statue she kept in her garden at home. After a while, the little mermaid realised that the young man was a Prince and that today was his birthday.

Greatly daring, the little mermaid swam closer to the big ship, her long tail gleaming silver in the light from its lanterns. But almost at once she dived beneath the waves as a shower of golden rockets shot up into the sky and the sea was suddenly aglow with a thousand flashing stars.

When the party was over and the ship was quiet and dark, the mermaid knew that it was time for her to return to her father's palace.

But she could not bear to leave the ship, so she swam round and round, delaying her moment of departure. Presently she saw dark storm clouds gather in the sky. The wind, too, began to rise and the waves suddenly were like swirling black mountains.

Sailors rushed on deck, hurriedly pulling down the great sails and setting the ship on a course that carried her over the waves. But, alas, at the height of the terrible storm, the main masts broke and the proud ship rolled over on her side.

The little mermaid swam anxiously among the wooden beams and the casks that floated on the angry waves. No earth man could live in such a raging sea. If she did not find the Prince she knew he would drown and she could not – must not – allow this to happen. The Princess heard the despairing cries of the sailors but she thought only of the Prince and when at last she found him, he was already half drowned.

Holding his head above the water, she swam with him towards the shore and then, with all her strength, pulled him on to the smooth golden sand. For a time, the little mermaid cradled the young earth man in her arms, completely happy as she looked down at him. Then she slipped away, back into the sea, to wait and watch.

As the dawn appeared, she saw the Prince stir and soon some pretty young girls came down to the beach. At the sight of the Prince, one ran back to the town for help and, presently, the Prince was lifted on to a litter and carried away.

Sadly, the mermaid dived quickly under the water and returned to her father's castle. Almost at once she went to her own special garden to be near the boy statue that reminded her so much of her handsome Prince.

As the days passed, the little mermaid grew more and more thoughtful and quiet. She rarely smiled and she refused altogether to join in her sisters' merry antics and games.

"Tell us your secret," her eldest sister begged her one day. "Perhaps we can help you."

"You cannot help me," the little mermaid said. "I have fallen in love with an earth man, a tall handsome Prince."

"But we know where the Prince lives!" cried the eldest sister. "We have often seen him in his sailing boat. Come, we will take you to his palace."

Then the sisters linked arms and rose up together through the sparkling sea. "There!" cried the eldest, as they lifted their heads above the waves. "There is his palace; it comes almost down to the water's edge. We dare not swim too close but the Prince often comes and stands on the marble steps that lead into the water."

For the first time for many days, the little mermaid smiled happily. "Now, I can come here whenever I wish," she said. "I am content for I know that one day I shall see him again."

Every morning after that, the little mermaid, rose up through the blue waters hoping to catch sight of the Prince. She swam closer to the land than any of her sisters would have dared and she came to know the fishermen and the times when the young Prince sailed his boat.

"How long do the earth people live?" the little mermaid asked her grandmother one day, as she combed out her golden hair.

"Not very long," said her grandmother. "But they do not die as we do. Why do you ask me again about such matters?"

"I do not want to become foam on the waves," said the Princess sadly. "I want to be like the earth people."

Her grandmother had no patience with such talk. "You are a sea maiden," she told the Princess sharply. "You have a fish-tail and you cannot expect to be accepted by the earth people. No earth man could ever love you because of your fish-tail – he would think it ugly."

That night the little mermaid sang more sweetly than ever for her father and her sisters. At the end of her song she slipped quietly away. Her mind was made up. She knew what she must do. She must visit the terrible sea-witch whose powers were known and feared throughout the sea kingdom.

No flowers grew where the sea-witch lived. There was nothing but deep dark whirlpools and the way was covered with black slimy mud. The sea-witch's house stood among tall twisting reeds that looked like fat yellow snakes. All around it were dangerous marshy swamps where only the poisonous creatures of the sea lived. So gloomy and terrifying was this place that the mermaid needed all her courage to swim towards the house.

She found the sea-witch sitting on a bench that was made out of the white bones of shipwrecked earth men. Snakes crawled over her arms and on her lap was her favourite pet, a fat ugly toad.

"I know what you want," said the sea-witch, as soon as the Princess swam up to her. "You want to get rid of your fish-tail and to have two supports so that the young earth Prince can fall in love with you."

"Yes, yes!" whispered the little mermaid. "That is what I want. Will you help me?"

"I will help you," said the sea-witch, "if you are willing to pay my price."

"I will pay it," said the Princess.

"Then I will prepare a magic potion which you must drink when you are on land," said the sea-witch. "Your tail will shrivel up and disappear and in its place you will have two legs. But there will be much pain. Are you willing to suffer?"

"Yes," whispered the mermaid.

"Whenever you walk it will be as if a sharp sword had pierced your feet," went on the witch. "But none will guess this for you will walk and dance with such grace that the eyes of the earth people will be dazzled by your beautiful movements."

"I am ready to endure the pain," said the mermaid. "What price must I pay for the gift of two legs?"

"You must give me your voice," said the witch. "It is the most beautiful voice in the sea kingdom, and I want it."

The Princess grew deathly pale. "But if I have no voice how can I tell the Prince of my love for him?" she asked quaveringly.

"Your eyes will tell him," said the sea-witch. "There will be no need for words. He will look into your eyes and see your love for him mirrored there."

"It is a high price," said the Princess at last, "but I am willing to pay it."

"So be it," said the witch. "But remember this. If you do not win the Prince's love and he marries someone else, your heart will break and you will, after all, become foam on the waves. You can never return to your father's castle."

"I understand," murmured the little mermaid. "I understand."

The witch brought out her black pot and began to make the potion that would change the mermaid into an earth girl. Many strange and horrible creatures she threw into the bubbling pot and the little mermaid covered her eyes so that she could not see the boiling mixture that steamed and hissed as the witch stirred and stirred. At last when the potion was ready, the witch dipped a small bottle into the pot and filled it with the liquid.

"There!" said the witch. "Take this bottle. Do not drink its contents until you are on land."

The mermaid took the bottle but she could not thank the witch for already her voice had gone. She was dumb.

Holding the bottle carefully, the little mermaid swam straight to the Prince's palace and dragged herself up on to the first step of the marble stairway where she had so often seen the Prince. Then she drank the witch's potion, draining the bottle to the very last drop.

It was just as the witch had said it would be. She felt terrible stabs of fearful pain as her fish-tail began to shrivel up. So great was the agony that the little mermaid could not bear it. She fainted. It was bright morning when she opened her eyes and saw the Prince himself standing over her. The Prince helped her up and the little mermaid, looking down, saw that she now had slim and white and very dainty little legs and feet.

The Prince was greatly taken with the little mermaid. He called her his little orphan from the sea, thinking that she had survived some shipwreck. When he found she could not speak, he petted her and made even more fuss of her, dressing her in pretty silk dresses and giving her golden slippers to wear on her tiny feet.

Soon, the little mermaid was everyone's favourite at court. When she danced, her movements were so graceful that they held the Prince spellbound. "Never have I seen such perfect dancing," he would say to her. And the little mermaid would look at him with eyes full of love, hiding the pain that pierced her feet like a sword whenever she took so much as a single step.

Day after day, the Prince kept the mermaid by his side. They walked together in the green forest or went riding among the hills. And never in all her life had the mermaid known such happiness. But although the Prince told her many times that he loved her, he loved her as he loved his small sisters. Not for one moment did he think of her as a wife.

One day the Prince told her that his counsellors were saying that soon he must think of choosing a wife. "I have no wish to marry," he laughed. "I have my dear little orphan of the sea to keep me company and dance for me. Why should I marry?"

The little sea Princess could only nod and smile and she tried to keep smiling when the Prince went on. "It seems," he said, "that the king of a neighbouring country has a very beautiful daughter who would make me a good wife. My Prime Minister says that it is my duty to visit this king and meet his daughter."

When the great ship that was to carry the Prince across the seas was fitted out, the Prince sent for the little mermaid. "I want you to come with me," he said. "I shall just take one look at this Princess and then return home. You will be my companion on the journey."

The little mermaid found it strange and wonderful to be sailing in a big ship across the ocean. Once, as she stood alone on the deck, she saw her five sisters come swimming through the water towards her. They looked up at her sadly and held out their white arms to her. But the little mermaid could not greet them with words. She could only smile and wave.

How anxiously she awaited the moment when the Prince would meet the new Princess face to face. Surely he would never be able to love her. Surely he would turn away and start making arrangements to return home. But, alas, when the mermaid saw the King's daughter waiting on the quayside to welcome the young Prince, she had to admit that this Princess was indeed beautiful. She was lovelier than any of the girls at the Prince's court.

By the end of the day, it was clear to everyone that the handsome young Prince was enchanted by the Princess. Not only was she very lovely but she was also kind and gracious and she was especially kind to the little mermaid.

After a few days, the Prince said to the mermaid, "I can see that you are growing to love the Princess. I know that already she loves you. When we marry, you shall live with us in the palace. Nothing will be changed."

For answer, the mermaid kissed the Prince's hand, hiding her eyes so that he would not see how her heart was breaking. She had failed to become his wife. The sea-witch had said that if the Prince married someone else, she would die. Soon she would be nothing more than white foam on the waves of the sea.

In great splendour, the Prince and the Princess were married and after the wedding, they went aboard the ship so that the Prince could take his new wife home to his own palace. The little mermaid went with them, hiding her sadness.

That night the mermaid did not sleep. So great was her sorrow it seemed as if her heart was breaking, and she knew that with the first rays of the sun she would die. As she stood all alone on the deck of the great ship, she suddenly saw her sisters rise out of the sea. They were pale as death and their long beautiful hair no longer streamed out behind them in the wind.

"We have given our beautiful hair to the sea-witch," the eldest called out, above the noise of the wind, "so that we might bring you help. You need not die tonight, after all. The witch has given us her silver knife and you must thrust it into the Prince's heart before the sun rises. The blood that falls on your feet will change them back once more into a fish-tail. You will become a mermaid again and will return to us."

The silver knife fell at the mermaid's feet and as she picked it up her sisters dived under the waves. Like a shadow, the mermaid stole into the Prince's cabin where he slept with his lovely bride at his side. For a moment the little mermaid stood there, holding the knife over his heart. Then she turned away and fled from the cabin. Far, far out to sea, she threw the witch's knife and as it sank beneath the waves, she dived from the side of the ship and followed it.

But the grave little mermaid did not, after all, change to white foam on the waves. Her gentle heart had won for her a special place among the good spirits of the air.

"Where am I going?" she asked, as she found herself floating gently upwards. And the spirits told her, "You are one of us now because you loved and suffered so much."

In the morning, the Prince searched in vain for his dear little companion. "It is strange," he told his young wife. "Although she is nowhere to be found on the ship, I feel that she is still with me."

"I am, I am," whispered the little mermaid as she tenderly brushed his brow. But only the wind and the sea knew that she had spoken.

The Giant's Three Golden Hairs

ONCE THERE was a poor woman who had always been unlucky but the day she gave birth to a baby boy her luck immediately changed for the better. To her great joy the wise woman of the village told her, "Your boy has a mark on his forehead which tells me he will be lucky all his life. What is more, when he has grown to manhood, he will marry the King's daughter."

Now, it was not long before the King himself heard of the wise woman's words and he was very angry. "I will never allow my daughter to marry a common village boy," he vowed. "That baby must die."

The village was not far from the King's palace so the very next day the King rode out to pay it a visit. Not wishing the poor woman to know that he was the King, he disguised himself as a nobleman.

He soon found the woman's cottage and went inside. The baby was in a cot and, as the King feared, he had a lucky mark on his brow. "That's a fine little boy you have," said the disguised King. "Give him to me and I will bring him up like a lord."

At first the poor woman refused. But the stranger offered her so much gold that she began to weaken. Then, at last, she picked up her baby and gave him to the noble, richly dressed man. "After all," she said, "no harm can come to my son for he has been born lucky and I would like him to become a great lord."

The King took the baby in his arms and rode out of the village. By and by he came to the river, where he put the child in a wooden box, nailed it up and threw it into the deepest part. Then the King returned to his palace, satisfied that he had destroyed the boy.

But the box did not sink. Instead it floated down the river until it was swept into the bank close to a mill. As luck would have it, the miller's apprentice was sitting on the bank eating lunch. When he saw the box, he pulled it towards him with a hook, certain that he was about to discover a great treasure. To his surprise, all he found was a baby boy who let out a yell as he was lifted out of the box.

The miller and his wife were delighted when they saw the baby. "We have no children of our own," said the miller's wife. "Let us keep this gift from heaven and bring him up as if he were our very own son."

So the poor woman's son was saved from the wicked King and he grew into a strong, handsome boy under the loving care of the miller and his wife.

When the boy was as tall as the miller and twice as strong, the King himself chanced to take shelter in the mill during a storm. He noticed the handsome youth and he congratulated the miller. "He is not really our son," the miller told him. "We do not even know his real name, though we call him Hans. You see, Sire, he was taken out of the river when just a baby. And, oh, what a lucky day that was for us!"

The King asked a few more questions but already he was certain that Hans was the very boy he had tried to be rid of. Hiding his dark thoughts, he said to the miller, "I would like to send a letter to the Queen for I will not see her for a few days. Let young Hans here be the messenger. I will reward him well and you shall have two gold pieces for yourself."

The miller willingly agreed. It was an honour to have Hans go to the palace and besides, he might make new friends who would help him to make his fortune. So the King quickly wrote a letter, sealed it, and gave it to Hans.

It was almost dark when Hans set out and after walking some time he was sure that he had lost his way. When he came to a big forest he saw just ahead of him a light coming from a cottage among the trees. "I might as well ask for shelter for the night," Hans thought. And he ran towards the cottage.

But the old woman who answered his knock shook her head when Hans asked if he might come in. "No, no, you can't stay here," she said. "My grandson is the leader of a band of robbers and they will kill you if they find you here."

"I'm not afraid," said Hans boldly. "I'm on my way to the palace with a letter for the Queen. But before I take another step I must have something to eat and somewhere to sleep." And he gave the old woman a friendly smile. "I'll take my chance with the robbers."

Hans had such a merry smile and such a friendly manner that the old woman had no wish to send him away. "Very well," she said at last. "I'll give you food and you can sleep on the floor until the robbers come home."

After Hans had eaten, he stretched out on the floor and was soon fast asleep. He was still sleeping when the robbers came back. "Don't be angry," the old woman said. "The boy will do us no harm."

The robber chief scowled and went over to kick Hans awake. Then he saw the letter addressed to the Queen on the floor beside the sleeping boy. "A letter to the Queen!" he exclaimed.

"That's right," said his grandmother. "The boy is taking the letter to the palace."

"Then I had better read it for myself," said the robber chief, bending down and picking up the letter. "What a strange letter this is," he told the old woman, as she began putting food on the table. "It's written in the King's hand and tells the Queen to kill the young man as soon as he hands over the letter. Well, we'll see about that."

Chuckling to himself, the robber sat down at the table and wrote another letter. *I want the bearer of this letter to marry our daughter right away*, wrote the robber, in a very fair imitation of the King's writing.

Then he tore up the first letter and put the second letter on the floor beside the sleeping Hans. "It's a good joke," he told his grandmother, "and it will serve that miserly King right."

Early the next morning, the robber chief wakened Hans, gave him breakfast of bread and honey and, with a show of kindness, put him on the road that would take him to the capital city. Then smiling merrily at the joke he had played on the King, he wished Hans good luck.

Hans thanked the robber chief and went on his way. That same morning he reached the city and was soon directed to the palace. The Queen received him warmly and read the letter. Then, somewhat to Hans' surprise, she planted a kiss on his cheek. "The King has commanded that you should marry my daughter without delay," said she. "It is all written in the letter."

As soon as Hans saw the beautiful Princess he was more than happy to agree for he fell in love with her immediately. The wedding was arranged for that same afternoon and there was much rejoicing.

Can you imagine the King's rage when he returned to the palace? "It was all written in your letter," protested the unhappy Queen. "I did just what you told me to do."

"It's a trick," stormed the King. "The letter was never written by me! That boy must go . . ." But the King had not counted on the Princess who was very much in love with Hans. "If he goes, then I go too," she told her father.

"Very well," said the King at last. "But he must pass a certain test if he is to remain your husband."

The Princess agreed, feeling certain that her brave new husband would be able to pass the hardest test her father could think of.

Now the King was both cruel and cunning and the test he set for Hans was indeed a hard one. "You must bring me back three golden hairs from the head of the Giant that lives in the caverns a hundred leagues from here," he told Hans.

"I'm not afraid of a Giant," Hans said boldly. "I'll set out at once."

Hans journeyed through pleasant valleys and over high mountains before at last he came to the first of the big towns through which he must pass before he could reach the Giant's cave. But when he stood before the gates of the town, a sentry barred his way.

"Why should I let you pass?" said the sentry. "What do you do?"

"I can do all things," Hans replied, with a merry smile. "And I know all things."

"Then tell me why our market fountain that once flowed with good red wine has become so dry that now we cannot even get water from it."

"Let me pass through your town," said Hans, "and I promise you I will give you the answer on my return journey."

Satisfied, the sentry opened the gates and allowed lucky Hans to pass through his town.

The next day Hans came to the second town that was also guarded by a sentry. "Why should I let you pass?" said the watchman. "What do you do?"

"I can do all things," answered Hans. "And I know all things."

"Then tell me why the tree in this town that used to have golden apples is now so bare that not a leaf is to be seen on its branches," said the watchman.

"Let me pass through your town," said Hans, "and I promise you I will give you the answer on my return journey."

"Very well," said the watchman. "Go on your way."

When Hans was almost within sight of the giant's cave he found he had to cross a deep wide river, and the only way to cross was by ferry. Hans asked the ferryman to row him across but the boatman refused. "Not until you have told me why I must always row backwards and forwards and am never able to leave this boat," said he.

"Take me across the river," said Hans. "And I promise you I will give you the answer on my return journey." And the ferryman agreed.

When Hans came, at last, to the huge dark cavern where the Giant lived, he entered boldly, quite prepared to ask the Giant for three of his golden hairs. But the Giant was not at home. Only the Giant's grandmother was there, rocking herself gently to and fro in a large rocking chair. Hans bowed respectfully to the old dame, thinking that she was not nearly as frightening as he would have expected. The Giant's grandmother took an instant liking to the handsome youth with his merry smile. "What do you want here?" she asked.

Hans told her his long story. "So you see," he ended, "if I do not return with three golden hairs from the Giant's head I will lose my beautiful wife and almost certainly my life as well."

"You will certainly lose your life if the Giant finds you here," said the old lady. "But I will help you if I can." And using her special magic powers, she changed Hans into a tiny ant. "Creep into the folds of my shawl," she said. "You will be safe there when my grandson comes home."

"That's very kind of you, ma'am," said Hans, not at all put out to find himself such a tiny insect. "But there are three things I must know or else my journey back to the palace will be impossible. I must know why a certain fountain that once flowed with red wine has now run dry. And why a tree that once had golden apples is now quite bare. Last of all, I must know why a certain ferryman must be for ever going backwards and forwards across the river and cannot leave his boat."

"These questions are not easy to answer," said the Giant's grandmother. "But my grandson knows most things. I will ask him tonight so listen carefully to all he says when I pull out the three golden hairs."

Later that night the Giant came home and the noise of his footsteps sounded like thunder as he entered the cave and flung himself into a great wooden chair. But presently he was on his feet again, roaring, "I smell, I smell, I smell a human . . ."

"Nonsense," said his grandmother sharply. "You smell your supper. Sit down again and eat." But the Giant was not satisfied and searched every nook and cranny of the vast cave before sitting down once more.

After his supper, the Giant, as was his custom, laid his huge head on his grandmother's lap and fell fast asleep. When he was snoring

loudly, the old woman bent over him and plucked a single golden hair from his head. The Giant woke at once. "Hey, Grandmamma, what are you doing?" he roared.

"I was dreaming," his grandmother told him. "And it was such a strange dream that I clutched at your hair."

"What was it? What did you dream?" asked the Giant sleepily.

"I dreamt that there was a fountain in a certain town that once flowed with wine and is now quite dry," said the old lady.

The Giant laughed. "Why, if they did but know it!" he exclaimed. "There is a big toad in the well of that fountain. If they got rid of the toad, the wine would flow again."

"Is that really so!" said the old woman. "Now go back to sleep."

Once again the Giant fell asleep and once again his grandmother pulled a golden hair from his head. This time the giant awoke with a roar of rage and his grandmother said quickly, "Don't be angry. I had another strange dream that caused me to pull at your hair. I saw a tree that was once heavy with golden apples and now is so bare that there is not even a leaf to be seen on its branches."

The Giant quickly forgot his anger as his grandmother stroked his golden hair. "Ah, Grandmamma," he said. "You did not dream long enough or you might have learnt what they must do. There is a little mouse gnawing at the roots of that tree. If they were to get rid of the mouse, the tree would bear golden apples once more."

The old lady smiled. "Go to sleep now," she said. "Perhaps this is the end to my dreaming." But grandmother knew that she must obtain a third golden hair and this she did when the night was all but finished. Jumping to his feet, the Giant scowled with rage as he rubbed his head. But his grandmother said softly, "How can you blame me if I dream so strangely that I clutch at your hair for comfort? Do you know, I dreamt I saw a poor ferryman rowing backwards and forwards for ever and quite unable to leave his boat."

Still angry the Giant grunted, "What a fool! All he has to do is to give one of his oars to the next man who sits in his boat. That will set him free while the other man must take his place . . ."

"How clever you are!" said the old lady. "Now I will make you a warm drink, for the night is almost over."

Early the next morning the Giant left the cave and as soon as he was gone the old lady took the ant out of the folds of her shawl and gave it back its human shape. "You are a child of luck," she told Hans. "I have here the Giant's golden hairs and already you know the answers to your questions. Go, before the Giant returns . . ."

Hans thanked her with all his heart, kissing her hand and promising he would always remember her. Then he placed the Giant's three golden hairs in his leather purse and set off for home.

When he found himself once again on the banks of the deep wide river, he told the ferryman, "I have the answer to your question, but first you must ferry me across to the far side." When Hans was safely on the bank, he called, "You can escape from your boat by giving the next man who sits in it one of the oars."

Presently Hans came to the town with the tree that would not bear golden apples. "Here is the answer to your question," he said to the sentry. "Rid yourself of a mouse that gnaws at the roots of the tree."

This was done immediately and the people of the town were so grateful when they saw the golden apples suddenly appear that they gave Hans two donkeys laden with bags of gold.

When Hans reached the next town, he told the sentry, "There is a huge toad in the well of your fountain. Rid yourself of the toad and your fountain will once again flow with good red wine."

This was done and the townsfolk, out of gratitude, gave Hans two more donkeys laden with gold and soon he was presenting himself at the palace.

"Here are the three golden hairs from the Giant's head," said Hans to the enraged King. Then he added, "I have not returned a poor man. Outside there is enough gold to build a palace as fine as this."

The greedy King began to look with more favour on Hans when he saw for himself that the young man had spoken truly. "Tell me," he said. "Where did you find all this gold and is there more of it?"

"Plenty," answered Hans. And he told the King how to find his way to the deep wide river. "Once there," he went on, "ask the ferry-man to row you across to the far bank. You'll find all the gold you can carry on the shore."

Well, that was the last Hans ever saw of the wicked King, who set out that same day on a long journey. But if by chance you come upon a deep wide river and see a ferryman with a crown upon his head, you'll know for certain what happened to him.

As for Hans, he was so lucky that the people thought he would make them a very good King. And they were quite right.

Little Tom Thumb

ONCE UPON a time there was a little boy who, when he was born, was no bigger than his father's thumb. So his father called him Tom Thumb and hoped that one day he would grow to be as big as his brothers. But, of course, he never did.

This story is all about little Tom Thumb and how he got the better of a cruel boy-eating ogre. It happened like this. Tom Thumb's father was a woodcutter. He was a good man but very poor and one winter, when the snow was on the ground, he found he had not enough money to buy a loaf of bread for his growing family.

"It's no use, wife," he said, one day. "Here we are with seven little mouths to feed and I can't make enough to buy a loaf of bread."

"We must manage somehow," said his wife. "There's one thing, Tom Thumb doesn't eat more than a sparrow."

"That's true," admitted her husband. "But his six brothers have big appetites and I cannot bear to sit here and watch them starve. No, wife, my mind is made up."

Well, husband and wife talked and talked until finally the woodcutter said what was in his mind. "As soon as the snow clears," he said, "I mean to take the boys deep into the forest and leave them there."

Now Tom Thumb had fallen asleep under his father's stool that night but when his mother began to weep and his father began to shout, he woke up. As he listened to them he soon realised what his father meant to do so he kept very still and quiet until both his parents left the room.

It was lucky for Tom's six brothers that he was so clever and that he could work out a plan to save them from being lost. As soon as the first sunny morning came along, Tom Thumb filled his pockets with small white stones. He guessed, you see, that this would be the morning his father would take them into the forest.

"Your father is going to take you into the forest today," their mother told the boys, and she gave them some hot milk. "You'll be able to play your games and have lots of fun." But she looked so sad and her eyes were so red that Peter, the eldest, asked, "If we're going to have fun why do you look so sad and why are your eyes red?" But their poor mother turned away, unable to answer.

Tom Thumb knew why, but he kept silent as his father told his sons to follow him into the forest. Well, they did have fun to begin with, playing hide-and-seek among the trees and running and jumping over the grass. But towards the end of the afternoon they were so tired that the woodcutter said, "We'll stop here for a rest. Build a fire and I will go further on to look for sticks."

The woodcutter walked away and Tom Thumb knew that he never meant to return. But he helped his brothers to start a fire, then he said, "Come on, boys! Let's sit round the fire and tell stories."

When it grew really dark and the owls began to hoot in the trees, Peter shivered, "I want to go home now," he said. "Why doesn't our father come back?"

"Perhaps the wolves have eaten him," said Johnny, who was the second youngest.

At the very idea of their father being eaten by wolves, all the boys except little Tom Thumb began to cry.

"What cry babies you are!" exclaimed Tom. "As soon as it is morning, we'll easily find our own way home and our father will be there to welcome us."

Comforted by their tiny brother's words, the others fell asleep and in the morning Tom showed them the little white stones he had dropped along the path as they had come through the forest. "We'll follow the stones," he told them. "They will show us the way back to our cottage."

Well, that is how clever Tom Thumb brought his brothers safely home. But soon after his father took the children into the forest again. Tom didn't have time to gather stones first. Instead he hastily snatched up some bread and this time he left a trail of breadcrumbs. Alas, the hungry forest birds ate the crumbs almost as soon as he let them fall.

This time the woodcutter took his children into a very dark part of the forest where the great trees grew so thickly together that they almost blotted out the sun. And soon he left them as he had done before. And this time they really were lost.

"We'll wait until morning," said Tom, as his brothers crowded round him. "Then we'll find our way back home just as we did last time."

But Tom Thumb had forgotten all about the hungry birds and when morning came he searched in vain for his trail of breadcrumbs. "Don't cry," he said to Peter, who was always the first to burst into tears. "We'll soon find a path that takes us home."

How dark and stormy it was as the children began to run through the trees! Then it started to rain and the rain blinded their eyes and made the forest grass so slippery that they were always falling down. At last, even brave little Tom began to lose heart. "I'll climb that tall tree over there," he said, trying to sound cheerful. "I'll be like a sailor climbing the mast of some big ship. The higher I climb the more I shall see."

His brothers watched as he clambered up the tall tree and they began to smile and throw their woolly caps in the air as suddenly they heard him shout: "Light ahoy! There's a house somewhere among the trees."

The boys crowded round him, as Tom clambered down. "Is it a light from our cottage window?" Peter wanted to know. But Tom shook his head.

"No," he said. "But that does not matter. We can ask for shelter and then tomorrow we will ask the way."

In good spirits, the brothers set off once again and now it didn't matter about the dark stormy sky or the heavy rain that beat down on their heads. But when, at last, they came upon the tall grey house that looked more like a castle, they were all very tired and soaked through to the skin.

With his brothers lined up behind him, Tom knocked on the great oak door. There was a long silence, then the door slowly opened and a tall thin woman stood looking down at them.

"Please," said Tom Thumb, "Can you give us something to eat and some shelter for the night?"

The woman shook her head. "You poor lambs," she said, "if I took you in now I would not be doing you a kindness. This is the house of a terrible ogre who is at present out hunting. No, no, get away from this place as fast as you can."

"I'm sorry, ma'am," said Tom, "but we're far too tired and hungry to go anywhere. If you don't take us in we shall all perish in this forest."

The woman hesitated. "I am the ogre's wife," she said at last. "I know my husband's ways. Why, if you were caught inside the house, it's more than likely he would eat you all one by one for his supper."

"We'll take that chance," said Tom. "Please let us come inside."

Now the ogre's wife was a kind-hearted woman even though she was married to a boy-eating ogre and Tom's little face, under his woolly cap, was so pleading that at last she opened the door a little more and said, "Very well. Come in, all of you. Perhaps there will be time for me to give you a bowl of hot porridge before the ogre comes home."

Tom followed the ogre's wife into a vast kitchen where a whole sheep was turning on a spit over a great fire. Then the woman sat them down at a long table and quickly put bowls of steaming porridge in front of them. How quickly they ate it up and how quickly, too, they began to smile and joke among themselves in the warm kitchen.

"I have always wanted pretty little boys of my own," the ogre's wife told them, as she filled up their bowls for a second time. "Alas, I have only seven great big ugly daughters who are already asleep upstairs. . ." she broke off, suddenly, at the sound of a thundering knock on the door. "It's – it's my husband," she whispered. "Quick – hide! Under that long couch over there!" As the boys ran to the couch, the woman cleared the table. Then straightening her apron, she went to the door and opened it.

As soon as the terrible ogre entered the kitchen he shouted for his supper. "It's quite ready, husband," said his wife. "You can see for yourself that the sheep is roasted and ready for eating."

The giant grunted as he sat down at table and his wife placed half the sheep in front of him. Presently, however, he raised his head and began sniffing. "Fee, fo, fum," he roared, "I smell – I smell. . ."

"You smell the roasting meat, that's all," said his wife quickly. "Now eat your supper while it is hot."

But the ogre was not satisfied. He searched the kitchen with his eyes until at last they became fixed on the couch. Then he rose to his feet, pushing the table away from him, and with two strides he was beside

the couch. One after another, he grabbed the boys and pulled them out.

"Oho!" he shouted. "So this is what you have hidden away, wife! Human boys – small and tender. How delicious they will be! Why, I have a good mind to eat you along with them, woman, except that your skin is yellow and wrinkled and would most likely taste unpleasant."

Tom Thumb on hearing these terrible words began begging for mercy. "Eat me, if you will," he said, "but spare my six brothers. They have done you no harm. And if you will only let them go you will never set eyes on them again."

The ogre laughed loudly at this. He held them up, one at a time in his great hands, then flung them into a corner. "Stay there," he said, "while I get my sharp hunting knife."

"Why not leave them until morning," said his wife. "Your supper is growing cold; there is no need for such haste."

Now the thought of the tender tasty meal that he could look forward to in the morning had put the ogre into a very good temper.

"You are right," he said. "I'll leave them until the morning. I'll have them roasted for my breakfast; that will give you time to make a really good sauce for them."

Tom Thumb sighed with relief when he heard these words and seeing that the ogre was no longer paying much attention to them, he whispered to the ogre's wife to take them out of the kitchen.

"You can sleep in the same room as my daughters," she told the boys. "There's a big double bed in their room which my husband keeps for his grandmother."

The ogre's seven daughter's were fast asleep in their own huge bed as Tom and his brothers entered the room. Tom saw, at a glance, how ugly they were with their hooked noses, cruel fang-like teeth and very big mouths. Indeed, they were so like their father that already they were beginning to eat little boys for breakfast too.

"My husband likes them to wear their gold crowns even when they are sleeping," the ogre's wife whispered, as she tucked the boys into the bed. "Do not talk among yourselves for I'm afraid my daughters, though still quite small, are nearly as fierce as their father."

Tom Thumb lay wide awake wondering how he could save his brothers who had cried themselves softly to sleep. "Supposing the ogre changes his mind," he suddenly thought," and comes upstairs with his sharp hunting knife to cut our throats. How shall we defend ourselves?"

Then he had a brilliant idea and, getting out of bed, he tiptoed over to the bed that held the ogre's sleeping daughters. Gently, oh so gently, he removed their crowns of gold and placed his brothers' woolly caps on their heads. Then, smiling to himself, he put their golden crowns on his brothers' heads. "Now if the ogre should come with his knife," he thought, "he will surely feel for the heads that wear the caps." Then, tired out, he fell fast asleep.

How long Tom Thumb slept he had no idea but he awoke to hear the clock downstairs strike midnight. Then he heard something else. Somebody terribly heavy was coming up the stairs. Under his weight each stair creaked and groaned as if they were complaining. "So I was right," Tom thought. "The ogre has changed his mind about eating us for breakfast. He's going to eat us now."

Presently, the door opened and Tom knew the ogre was in the room, but it was so dark that the giant had to feel his way around. He was very sleepy and very slow as he came into the room for he had drunk a great deal of wine with his supper. When he came to the bed where Tom lay with his brothers, the ogre stretched out a huge hand and touched – what do you think – the golden crowns!

"Wrong bed!" he grunted. "M-must be the other!" And he stumbled clumsily across the room. Although he felt more than usually sleepy, he remembered quite clearly that the boys had been wearing bright woolly caps. When his groping fingers felt something soft and warm he muttered, "Right bed! Woolly caps! Now I've got the rascals!"

He raised his knife and, oh dear me, he cut off the heads of his seven sleeping daughters! This deed done, the ogre gave a mighty yawn and then decided that really he was far too sleepy to enjoy a meal at such a late hour. "I'll leave my wife to see to it in the morning," he told himself, as he left the room.

No sooner had he gone than Tom Thumb sprang from the bed. "Wake up! Wake up!" he whispered to his brothers. "We must escape now. Tomorrow will be too late."

His brothers woke at once, shivering and frightened. "Follow me," Tom told them. "The ogre's gone to bed. He thinks we're dead so he is no longer on his guard.

Then he led his brothers downstairs and out of the back door. As silent as mice, they crept through the garden and climbed over the wall.

"Now we must run," said Tom. "We must run and run as fast as we can until we are far away from this terrible place."

The brothers ran as fast as their trembling legs would carry them all through the night, stopping only for short rests. They didn't dare sit down for long.

Meanwhile, as soon as it was light the ogre awoke and began to

think, with pleasure, of the feast that he was soon to have. "Go upstairs and get the boys ready," he told his wife. And his wife, not knowing the sight that was to meet her eyes, obeyed. When she saw what had happened to her seven daughters, she screamed loudly. Her screams soon brought the ogre into the room, and one glance was enough to show him how he had been tricked into killing his own daughters.

"Where did they get these woolly caps?" asked the wife stupidly. But the ogre was in too much of a rage to answer. "I'll catch them, never fear!" he shouted. "Fetch me my seven-league boots."

The ogre had won his seven-league boots in battle and they were more precious to him than the bags of gold he kept under the floor-boards. They were magic, you see, and could carry whoever wore them seven leagues – which is a very long way – with a single stride.

In his wonderful boots, the ogre strode up and down the forest searching in vain for Tom Thumb and his brothers. Then he left the forest and strode up and down the countryside and he was such a terrifying sight that everybody ran indoors and hid under their beds.

Now it is a very well known fact that anyone who wears seven-league boots grows tired very easily and by the end of the morning the ogre was quite worn out. He was also very angry that he was taking so long to catch the boys. In fact he was so furious that he got very short of breath and so, to give himself a bit of a rest, he sat down close to a huge rock.

Tom Thumb and his brothers were short of breath too and they had chosen that very rock to shelter under while Tom Thumb kept a look-out.

"Don't move or speak," Tom whispered, when he saw the ogre.

His brothers were too scared to do anything except huddle together. But not Tom Thumb! As soon as he saw the ogre close his eyes and begin to doze, he crept out of his hiding-place and climbed the nearest tree. There, to his great joy, was his father's cottage. It was so close that he could see the smoke from the chimney curling up into the sky.

"We're nearly home," he whispered to his brothers, when he returned to them. "As soon as the ogre begins to snore, you must creep out of this hiding place, up that short hill behind you and then down the other side. Promise me you'll do that. Our father's cottage is at the bottom of the hill. You'll be safe there."

Then little Tom Thumb, not a bit afraid, went up to the sleeping ogre and gently pulled off his boots. Now the boots being magic always fitted their wearer so when Tom put them on they shrank to a tiny size.

In his seven-league boots Tom Thumb covered the miles back to the ogre's house in a flash. When the ogre's wife saw him standing at the door, wearing her husband's magic boots, she almost fainted away. But little Tom Thumb pretended not to notice her white face. "I have come from your husband, ma'am," he said, smiling cheerfully. "These boots are proof of that. He has been taken prisoner and needs his bags of gold to buy his freedom. He gave me his boots so that I could come to you quickly."

The ogre's wife was so upset at the thought of losing her husband as well as her daughters, that she did not stop to ask herself how he had been taken prisoner when before no one had dared even to speak to him. She gave Tom the bags of gold that were hidden under the floorboards and begged him to return quickly with news of her husband.

Tom made straight for his father's cottage and was there more quickly than you and I can say 'cock robin'. What a welcome he got and what praise his brothers gave him as they told all over again how he had saved them from the wicked ogre.

Then Tom Thumb threw the bags of gold on the table. "All our troubles are over," he cried. "This gold will make us rich for the rest of our lives."

Now those who know the woodcutter's family very well say that Tom Thumb gave the gold to the King for, as his mother said, it had most likely been stolen from the King and his subjects. Others say he took it back, in secret, to the ogre's wife and told her to hide it away for her old age.

Almost certainly Tom Thumb did not keep the gold after all, but then he had no need of it for the King made him the Court's Royal Messenger. Thanks to his magic boots, Tom Thumb was a great success in his new position. Soon he was given the title of Baron and a hundred gold pieces which he gave to his father.

In time, Tom Thumb became such a favourite at Court that the King invited him to live in his palace. Tom Thumb agreed, but he never grew too proud for his family whom he visited every week so that he could see for himself they had everything they needed.

The Garden of Paradise

ONCE UPON a time there was a King's son who, when he was very young, loved listening to stories. His grandmother told him the best stories of all and the one he liked to hear over and over again was about the Garden of Paradise.

"The Garden of Paradise," she would say, "is the most beautiful place you can imagine. Every flower is a delicious little cake and on some, the history of the world is written. You have only to eat one of these little cakes and you know your history lesson from A to Z."

At the time, the small boy believed this. But as he grew older, he heard about Adam and Eve, the man and woman who first lived in the Garden of Paradise, and he understood that it was not exactly as his grandmother had described.

As he grew older the King's son loved books more than anything and by the time he was seventeen he had a huge library of splendid books. Day after day he searched in them for mention of the Garden of Paradise but although they told him many things about the world, they said nothing of the Garden which filled all his thoughts.

One day, as he walked alone in the forest, the sky suddenly grew dark with heavy black clouds. Then it began to rain so heavily that it poured down on him like a great river, soaking him through and

117

through. The Prince had wandered away from the familiar paths and by nightfall he was lost. Stumbling and slipping over the moss-covered stones and faint with weariness and hunger, he came at last upon an enormous cave.

In the middle of this cave a huge fire burnt and there, on a spit, was a big stag slowly turning round and round. Beside the fire sat a woman, so tall and strong that it seemed to the young Prince she could have been a man. When she saw him, she called out, "Come nearer. Come and sit by the fire and dry your clothes."

"Thank you," said the Prince, and he entered the cave and sat down beside her on the ground. "When the storm came so suddenly I lost my way in the forest."

"You are now in the Cavern of the Winds," said the woman, as she threw some logs on the fire. "I am the mother of the Four Winds. They will be home presently."

"What do they do, these four sons of yours?" asked the Prince curiously.

"They are in business on their own account up there with the clouds," the woman answered gruffly, and once again the Prince thought how different she was from any of the women at his father's court.

As if reading his thoughts, the woman went on, "You do not understand. I am their mother and I must be strong to keep them in order for my sons are wild fellows. Do you see those four sacks hanging on the wall?"

The Prince looked at the big sacks and nodded. "I saw them at once," he said, "as soon as I came into the cave."

"My sons are afraid of those sacks," laughed the mother of the Four Winds. "When they do wrong I bend them and pop them into the sacks. There they must stay until I choose to let them out. They know well enough what will happen to them if they disobey me or anger me."

"When will your sons return?" asked the Prince, after a long silence.

"Here comes one now," she cried, as there was a sudden rush of icy cold wind. "Here he is. Here is my eldest, the North Wind."

The Prince shivered with cold as the North Wind came into the cave. What a huge fellow he was, dressed in bears' skins and with long icicles hanging from his beard. His cap and boots were of sealskin and he was covered with snowflakes.

"Don't go too near the fire," the Prince cried out in alarm. "You'll get frost-bite!"

But the giant North Wind only laughed, a deep, bellowing roar, as he looked down at the Prince. "What's this mannikin doing here?" he asked his mother.

"He lost his way," his mother told him, "and now he is my guest. If you do not treat him kindly you will have to go into the sack."

And she threw more wood on the fire. "Now tell us where you have been."

"I've been to the Polar Seas," said the North Wind, no longer laughing at the mention of the sack. "I've been to Bear's Island with the walrus hunters. I blew away the mist that hung over the hunters' house that they had built of ship-wrecked wood and covered with walrus skins. And I teased the polar bear that growled at me. Then I blew my ships, the great icebergs, until they crushed the tiny man-made boats in which sat the men-harpoonists. I covered them with snowflakes and drove them out to sea. They won't come near Bear's Island again."

"That was a wicked thing to do," scolded his mother. "I'll hear no more of your story."

"I'll say no more then," replied the North Wind, glancing nervously at the sacks. "Here comes my little brother from the west."

The Prince thought the West Wind looked like a wild man of the forests as he rushed into the cavern carrying a heavy club and wearing a broad-brimmed hat that came down over his eyes. His mother smiled at him and asked him where he had been.

"I've come from the green forests," he said, "where the water snakes lie in the wet grass and the wild buffalo swim in the rivers. I chased the wild ducks and I blew a storm so that the old trees crashed down and broke into splinters. I really enjoyed myself today."

Presently, as they talked, the South Wind arrived. He wore a turban on his head and a flowing cloak around his shoulders which reminded the Prince of pictures of desert travellers he had seen in his books at home.

"How cold it is in here," cried the South Wind, and he threw more wood on the fire. "That's my big brother's fault."

"Nonsense," said the North Wind. "It's so hot in here you could roast a polar bear."

"Stop!" ordered their mother, pointing to the sacks. "I want to hear your story, South Wind. Where have you come from?"

"Africa," said the South Wind. "I ran races with the ostriches and when I came to the desert I met a caravan. The people were just about to kill their last camel to get water. So I blew the soft yellow sand into whirling pillars and I covered them all, camel and caravan, with the sand. It was fun. One day I'll go back and blow the sand away and take a look at their white bones. . ."

"Wicked fellow!" cried his mother angrily. "You have done nothing but evil." And she seized the South Wind round the body and popped him into one of the sacks, before he could utter a sound.

"Your sons certainly are wild men," remarked the young Prince. "What of the East Wind? Is he like his brothers?"

"You may judge for yourself," said the mother of the Winds softly, as the East Wind entered the cavern.

The Prince saw that the East Wind was shorter than his brothers and that he was dressed like a Chinaman.

"So you have been in China," said his mother fondly. "I thought you were going to the Garden of Paradise."

"I fly there tomorrow," said the East Wind. "It will be a hundred years tomorrow since I was last there. In China I had only time to whistle through the bamboo forests and ring all the bells in the big cities. But it was fun!"

"You are foolish," said the old woman. "I am glad you are going to the Garden of Paradise tomorrow. You may learn some sense. Bring me home a small bottle filled with the water from the Spring of Wisdom."

"I will," said the East Wind. "But let my brother, the South Wind, come out of the sack. He must tell another story about the Phoenix bird so that I can tell it to the Fairy Queen in the Garden of Paradise. She always wants to hear about the Phoenix bird."

"Very well," said his mother. "I love you best of all and it's hard to refuse you anything."

The Prince smiled when he saw the South Wind creep out of the sack like a naughty schoolboy. "I can tell you about the Phoenix bird," he said. "I have read about him in some of my books at home. He came out of an egg that lay in a burning nest. It was red hot because his mother had set herself and the nest on fire."

"You are right," said the South Wind. "There is only one Phoenix bird left in the world. The last time I met him he gave me this palm leaf for the Princess."

"She will like that," said the East Wind, taking the leaf.

The Prince stared at the East Wind with eager interest. "Tell me about the Garden of Paradise," he cried. "Where does it lie?"

"Do you want to go there?" asked the East Wind, as he began to eat some of the roasted deer his mother gave him.

"With all my heart," answered the Prince.

"You have heard of Adam and Eve, I suppose," continued the East Wind. "Well, when they were driven out of the Garden, it sank into the earth. It is still wonderfully beautiful but now the Queen of the Fairies lives there. Sit on my back tomorrow and I will take you there if you wish."

After their supper, the brothers lay down to sleep and the Prince lay down beside them. Soon he, too, was fast asleep. When he next opened his eyes, it was early morning and to his surprise he found that he was sitting on the East Wind's back and flying high above the clouds. If the East Wind had not been holding on to his arms, he would almost certainly have toppled off.

"You didn't give me a chance to thank your mother or say farewell to your brothers," said the Prince at last. "I am sorry about that."

"I wanted to make an early start," said the East Wind. "We have a very long way to go before we reach the Garden of Paradise." And he flew on and on, over forests and high mountains and across vast seas.

As it grew dark, the East Wind said, "Hold tight, for now we are coming to the highest mountains in the world. Then soon we shall come to the Garden of Paradise."

"I'm glad to hear it," said the Prince, who was tired of hanging on. "It seems that the air is beginning to smell more sweetly as if it were scented with flowers and spices."

"You're right," the East Wind told him. "We are now quite close

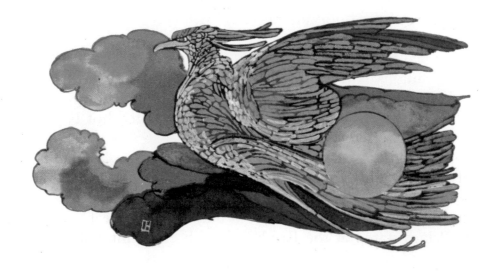

to the Garden." And he began to drop out of the sky, flying lower and lower until at last he landed on soft green grass. The Prince jumped off his back and stretched himself thankfully.

"How beautiful it is!" he exclaimed. "The grass is so green and the flowers all the colours of the rainbow."

"We have not yet arrived at the Garden," said the East Wind. "We must pass through that huge cave you see there in front of you where the vines hang like green curtains. That is the way to the Garden of Paradise."

What a strange cave it was! To begin with the Prince found it icy cold and he began to shiver violently. A few steps later and it was warm, bathed in brilliant sunshine. Great blocks of stones, curiously shaped, stood along the walls of the cavern and sometimes the passage was so narrow that the Prince had to squeeze and push his way forward. Then, at last, he saw just ahead of him the most wonderful blue sky.

The air was filled with the scent of roses as the Prince left the cavern and came to a halt beside a clear river where little fishes, silver and gold, flashed in and out among coloured stones that glistened like jewels. A marble bridge spanned this river and the East Wind led him across. "We are now on the Island of Happiness," said he, "where the Garden of Paradise lies."

"How wonderful!" cried the Prince. "Everything is so much more

beautiful than I ever imagined." And he smiled with pleasure as he looked about him and saw the strange delicate flowers, the climbing plants and green vines.

A flock of peacocks, their trains spread out like brilliant fans, walked towards him. And then he saw among the trees, antelopes and tigers, so tame that the wild wood pigeons were perching on their backs. Scarcely able to breathe for wonder and happiness, the Prince lost all count of time.

Presently, as he stood there, the Fairy Queen of Paradise appeared. She was young and very beautiful with a star in her long golden hair. The East Wind greeted her like a friend and he gave her the palm leaf from the Phoenix bird. Then he turned to the Prince. "He is a friend of mine," he smiled. "Will you take care of him?"

And the Fairy took the Prince's hand and led him into her palace. In the middle of the vast marble hall where the Prince found himself, he saw a tree, tall and straight, and heavy with shining golden apples.

"Is this the Tree of Knowledge?" he asked, knowing that it must be, and the Fairy Queen nodded and smiled.

"Can – can I always stay here?" he asked, his eyes bright with happiness. "It is what I desire most in the world!"

"That depends on yourself," answered the Fairy. "You must do what I tell you. If you disobey, all will be lost."

"I will be strong," cried the Prince. "I will take nothing that is forbidden."

"The East Wind leaves tonight," said the Fairy. "He will not return for a hundred years. That is a long time to wait."

"It will pass quickly," said the Prince. "Please let me stay."

"If you do," replied the Fairy, "every evening when I leave you I shall have to call to you, 'Come with me'. But you must not obey. You must stay where you are."

"I understand," the Prince said eagerly. "I promise I will not try to follow you."

"I will do all in my power to persuade you to come to me," said the Fairy Queen. "If you do follow me, you will find me under the Tree of Knowledge. Bend down and kiss me and the Garden of Paradise will sink into the earth and be lost to you for ever."

"I promise I will not come to you," declared the Prince. "No matter how often you call me."

Then the East Wind appeared and said, "We shall meet here in a hundred years. Take good care of yourself." And he spread out his broad wings and flew away.

For the rest of that wonderful day the beautiful Fairy Queen stayed with the Prince, dancing with him among the flowers, and sitting beside him under the green trees. When the sun went down, she led him into a room filled with white and golden lilies and some of her maidens brought him fruit to eat and wine to drink.

"Now," said she, "it is time for me to leave you." But as she left the room, the Prince could hear her gentle voice calling, "Come with me! Come with me!" And forgetting his promise, he rushed after her.

When he came to the great hall where the Tree of Knowledge stood, he saw her, lying on a bed of leaves, under its spreading branches. And, although her eyes were closed as if in sleep, she was smiling. She was so beautiful that the Prince could not stop himself from bending down and kissing her.

Immediately there was a fearful clap of thunder – so loud and terrifying that the Prince fell to the ground in terror, his eyes closed. When next he opened them, a cold rain was beating down on his face and he was shivering as if he had a fever. He struggled to his feet and saw that he was in the forest close to the Cavern of the Winds. Then he saw the mother of the Winds and she looked at him fiercely. "You

have failed," she said. "And on your very first evening! If you were a son of mine I would put you into the sack!"

"Yes, I have failed," said the Prince sadly. "I have lost everything. Shall I ever get a second chance?"

"Who knows?" said the mother of the Winds. And she went into the cave, leaving him alone in the forest.

What do you think happened to the Prince? Some say he wandered the world for a hundred years searching for the Garden of Paradise which he could never find. But others say that the East Wind took pity on him and carried him there on his back so that, after all, he could have a second chance.

Three Little Men of the Forest

ONCE UPON a time there lived an old shoemaker, whose wife had died. A year or so later, the shoemaker thought to himself, "I might as well marry again." The truth was that he had recently met a widow who also wished to marry.

Now the shoemaker had one lovely daughter called Catherine, and the widow had a plain daughter called Hilda. And the shoemaker hoped that the two girls would be friends. But the girls were as different as chalk is from cheese. Catherine was as gentle and kind as she was pretty, and Hilda – well, sad to say, Hilda was as mean and disagreeable as she was plain.

The shoemaker married the widow at the beginning of winter and as the weeks passed his new wife grew to hate her gentle step-daughter. She hated her all the more when she saw her own daughter sitting beside her for then she could see with half-an-eye who was the prettiest.

As winter set in, the river was frozen as hard as stone and the valley was covered with snow. And it was then that the shoemaker's wife made a cloak out of paper for Catherine before sending her out into the bitter cold. "Fetch me a basketful of wild strawberries for nothing else will satisfy me," she told the girl. "And don't dare come back until you have found them."

"But the ground is frozen hard and the snow covers everything," poor Catherine cried, as she took the paper cloak and the basket. "Do you want me to freeze to death?"

For answer, her stepmother opened the door and pushed her out into the snow. "And see that your basket is full," she shouted, before slamming the door shut.

Catherine made for the forest where every blade of grass was hidden by the snow. There was not a strawberry to be seen and, at last, shivering with cold, she came to a cottage right in the middle of the woods. Here, three little Dwarfs lived and when they saw the girl at the door, they called out to her to come inside. Then they seated her by their fire, took off her paper cloak and asked if she had anything to eat in her basket.

"I have only a slice of bread," she answered. "That was all my stepmother would give me. But I will gladly share it with you." And she broke the bread into four tiny pieces and gave each of the Dwarfs a mouthful.

"What brings you into the forest on such a day?" one of the little men asked after they had eaten her bread.

"I must fill my basket with wild strawberries," Catherine said. "Thank you for taking me in. But now I must try once again to find some."

"We would like you to help us first by sweeping away the snow with this broom from our back door," said another of the Dwarfs, as Catherine rose to go. "Will you do that for us?"

"Of course I will," said Catherine, thinking that she would like to help such friendly little men. "It won't take long." And she took the broom and went outside.

When she had gone, the tallest of the Dwarfs whispered, "What can we give her? She has shared her bread with us and now she is sweeping away the snow."

"I'll grant that she becomes more beautiful every day," said the youngest and fattest of the Dwarfs.

"I'll grant that a piece of gold falls out of her mouth with every word she speaks," said the middle Dwarf.

"And I'll grant that a King's son shall come along and fall in love with her," said the tallest of the Dwarfs.

Then they fell silent as Catherine rushed into the room, her face alight with happiness. "Look!" she cried. "Look, what I found as I swept away the snow. Lovely red strawberries!" And she held up her basket.

The three little men showed no surprise. Instead they wished her a pleasant journey home and as she ran down the path, they stood in the doorway and waved her goodbye.

Her stepmother, when she saw the strawberries, gave her no thanks but scolded her for taking so long. "I found a little cottage..." Catherine began and stopped for a shower of gold pieces had fallen out of her mouth and was lying at her feet.

"Goodness!" cried Hilda, who happened to come into the room.

"Whatever next! She's throwing gold about as if it was sugar! I suppose you just happened to find a bag of it in the forest?"

At this, Catherine, with some difficulty, told the whole story and by the end of it a fortune in gold pieces lay at her feet.

"Give me my cloak and let me go immediately into the forest," Hilda said to her mother, when Catherine had gone upstairs. "I'll find that cottage, and the Dwarfs will do the same for me as they have done for her."

So then her mother wrapped her daughter in a warm fur cloak, packed her basket with bread, meat and cake and allowed her to go into the woods.

Hilda found the cottage without any difficulty and knocked on the door. The three little men called out to her to enter. Then they seated her by the fire, took off her warm fur cloak and asked her if she had anything to eat in her basket.

"I have," said Hilda, who had, so far, not spoken a word of thanks.

"Will you share your food with us?" asked the tallest of the Dwarfs.

"Certainly not," snapped the girl. "I have scarcely enough to satisfy my own hunger." And with that she took the bread and meat out of her basket and began to eat it quickly. Then she ate the cake while the three little men silently watched her.

As soon as she had eaten the last crumb, they said to her. "Will you sweep away the snow from our back door? Here is a broom."

"Do your own sweeping," retorted Hilda rudely. "I'm not your servant!" And she tossed the broom into a corner. "Now," she continued, "I'll go outside and look for these wild strawberries that my stepsister found in your garden." And she clattered out of the cottage.

When she was gone, the Dwarfs said to each other, "What shall we give her? She is so rude and has such bad manners that we cannot wish her well." Then the tallest Dwarf said, "I'll grant that she grows more ugly every day." And the middle Dwarf said, "I'll grant that with every word she speaks a toad will drop out of her mouth." This, as you may know, is a favourite punishment of all dwarfs and fairies.

And the third and fattest of the little men said, "I'll grant that, one day, she gets a soaking in the river."

Hilda searched in vain for the strawberries and without bothering to thank the little men for allowing her to sit by their fire, she returned home in a very bad temper. Imagine her mother's fright when, with her very first angry words, three toads dropped from her mouth and began hopping over the kitchen floor!

Now, more than ever, Catherine was hated by her stepmother and the next day she gave her a net and an axe. "Take this net," she said, "and go to the pond. Cut a hole in the ice with the axe and drag the net through the water so that you may catch a fish. Don't dare to come home without any fish."

Poor Catherine's face was blue with cold and her fingers numb as

she ran to the pond, dragging the heavy net behind her. With the axe she cut a hole in the ice and then pulled the net through the water. But not a single fish did she catch.

Again and again she tried and was just about to give up when she heard the sound of horses' hooves on the road that ran beside the pond. She looked behind her and there was the King's carriage coming along at a rattling pace.

The young King stopped his carriage when he saw the beautiful young girl on the ice and beckoned her to come to him. "What are you doing?" he asked curiously.

"I must drag this net in the water and catch some fish," Catherine told him, a shower of gold pieces falling on the ice as she spoke.

Who knows if it was the gold or Catherine's gentle beauty that first attracted the handsome young King? At any rate he quickly invited her to ride with him back to his palace and by the end of the journey he was more than a little in love with her and she with him. And the very next day they were married.

A whole year passed in great happiness, particularly for the King, for Catherine not only grew more beautiful with every day but was forever dropping gold pieces which she gave him to spend on the poor people in his kingdom.

At the end of the year, a fine baby son blessed their marriage and the three little men of the forest came to the grand Christening Party, though they said not a word about their previous good wishes for the gentle Catherine.

As for the old shoemaker, in time he grew so weary of his nagging wife and ugly stepdaughter, who seemed to grow uglier every day, that, at last, he pushed them both into the river. "Don't ever come back," he shouted after them, as they scrambled up the far bank. "I'm sick and tired of you both *and* the toads. . ."

When the shoemaker found himself all alone, he made his way to the palace where he was joyfully received by his daughter. She gave him a splendid suite of rooms and a servant of his own and he stayed with her for the rest of his days and was very happy.

Ricky-of-the-Tuft

ONCE UPON a time there was a Queen who gave birth to a very ugly baby boy. Indeed, some of the ladies of the court vowed secretly that he was the ugliest baby in the whole world! The reason for his ugliness was a strange little tuft of hair that sprouted, like grass, out of the top of his head. Of course, no one dared to say how ugly he was in the presence of the Queen but she knew very well her baby was not nearly as pretty as others.

Now, although the baby was christened Richard, he soon became known as Ricky-of-the-Tuft which upset the Queen very much. At last she sent for the wisest fairy in the land.

"I cannot change the way your baby looks," said the wise fairy. "But I can give him a special gift. He will grow up to be very wise and very clever. What is more, if he falls in love with a stupid girl he will be able to give her some of his wisdom and cleverness."

Well, Ricky grew up and he was so wise and so clever that no one noticed his short legs, his long nose or the odd tuft of hair that sprouted out of his head.

One day an artist came to the palace and showed him a portrait of a most beautiful Princess. "She is indeed lovely," said Ricky. "I should very much like to meet her."

Then the artist told Ricky a strange story about the beautiful Princess who lived in a neighbouring kingdom. "When she was born," said the artist, "she was said to be the most beautiful baby in the whole world. Her mother was so proud of her that she boasted to everyone about her beautiful new baby daughter. One day a wise fairy came to the palace to see the child and the proud Queen boasted to her too."

"A wise fairy came to see me when I was a baby," said Ricky, as he gazed at the picture.

"This fairy decided to punish the proud Queen," went on the artist. "She told her that the child would grow up to be very stupid. And the truth is, sire, that she is so stupid and so dull that no man wants to stay in her company for long. She can scarcely put four words together and so she is left very much alone."

Ricky gave the artist a great deal of money for the Princess's picture and in the weeks that followed spent much of his time standing in front of it, just gazing. At last he made up his mind to visit the lovely Princess and, if she were as beautiful as her picture, ask her to marry him.

As luck would have it, almost as soon as he had crossed the border into the neighbouring kingdom, he came upon the Princess. She was walking in her favourite woods where she could be alone and far away from people who knew her to be stupid. And she looked so lonely and sad that Ricky's kind heart was immediately touched.

"You are three times more beautiful than your portrait," he told her, as he went up to her. "My name is Prince Ricky-of-the-Tuft and I have long wished to meet you."

The poor Princess was completely at a loss for words. She blushed and stammered and only managed to say, "I thank you." Then she stopped altogether.

"I know who you are," Ricky went on in his gentle voice. "And I want you to know that I love you."

"Alas," said the Princess, after a long silence. "I am the most stupid girl in the whole world. No man wants to stay with me for I have nothing to say . . ."

This was a very long speech for the Princess to make and she sank on to the grass and hid her face in her hands.

Ricky sat down beside her and presently the Princess found enough

courage to look at him properly. His ugly face gave her some courage and she spoke again. "I have a sister," she told Ricky, "who is very plain, but she is so witty and clever that already she has had ten proposals of marriage."

"What would you give to be as clever and witty as your sister?" asked Ricky.

"Anything," answered the Princess. "All my beauty. . . ."

"If you could bring yourself to take me for your husband," said Ricky eagerly, "I could give you this gift of cleverness that you want so much."

The Princess plucked at the grass quite unable to make sense of what the odd little man was saying. But when Ricky repeated his words slowly and clearly, she looked up.

"You m-mean I c-could be clever?" she asked. "How? When?"

"You have only to promise to marry me," said Ricky, "and the gift is yours."

"I promise, I promise!" cried the Princess, her blue eyes shining. Then she added, "But not right away. . . ."

"Of course not," said Ricky. "I will give you a whole year to think about it. A year from now I will meet you in these same woods and ask you to keep your promise."

As Ricky stood up and pulled her to her feet, the Princess felt a powerful change come over her. Suddenly she found herself able to speak in a commanding and clever way. Words poured out of her mouth. She began to tell Ricky about her father and the laws he had passed to make his people happy.

Ricky-of-the-Tuft listened quietly, a smile on his ugly face. "Truly you are clever," he said. "You now have the gift I promised you. Go back to your father's palace and see how things will change."

Then, bowing low, he left her. The Princess ran all the way home. As soon as she was back in the palace she called the servants together and told them how they could perform their duties much faster if they followed the advice she was about to give them. They listened in amazement. Until that moment, they had looked upon the Princess as hopelessly stupid and treated her like a child.

That night, at dinner, the Princess talked with so much sense about the affairs of the kingdom that the King quite forgot to eat as he listened. As for the Queen, she was so delighted at her daughter's new-found cleverness that she almost fainted with joy.

Soon, the palace was crowded with handsome young men all begging the Princess to look upon them with favour. Day after day she astonished the people with her wisdom, and poets and writers recorded her sayings for posterity.

A whole year passed. The Princess knew that one day she must choose a husband from all the handsome young noblemen who came to the palace. But she could not make up her mind about any one of them. They all seemed equally handsome and equally pleasant. At last, to escape their attentions, she left the palace and went into the woods.

As she wandered among the trees, she was suddenly astonished to hear voices: "Frizzle the fry: Pit the pancake: Dip the dough."

"What nonsense is this?" thought the Princess, unable to make any sense out of the words that came to her ears. "And where can these voices be coming from?"

To her amazement, as she took a step forward the ground in front of her opened up and she found herself staring down into a vast, underground kitchen.

Little tiny men, no more than dwarf-height, were rushing hither and thither in tall hats and white aprons that reached to their feet.

Others, dressed all in green, were laying a long polished table with golden goblets and plates of gold and silver. Some of the little men were singing while they stirred the boiling pots and mixed dough, and some were making garlands of brightly coloured flowers and leaves.

"Now, what can all this be about?" the Princess asked herself.

Presently, as she watched, several of the little men clambered up a long rope ladder and began gathering more leaves from the ground where she stood. They paid no attention to her and the Princess was forced to bend down and take one firmly by the arm. "Tell me," she said, "what are you all doing?"

"Don't you know?" said the little dwarf. "We are preparing a wedding feast for our friend and master, Ricky-of-the-Tuft. Our Prince is going to marry a beautiful Princess tomorrow and we want everything to be ready in time."

"Ricky – Ricky-of-the-Tuft!" the Princess repeated the name to herself, as she let go of the little man. Suddenly, she remembered her promise and all that had passed between Ricky and herself just a year ago.

If there had been time, the Princess would have run from the woods. But it was too late for as she turned she saw Prince Ricky himself coming towards her. He was so richly and finely dressed that it looked indeed, as if he was going to a wedding!

"So you have remembered!" he exclaimed with a happy smile. "You have come to keep your promise."

"I have not!" cried the Princess, looking at the ugly little man with scorn. "That promise was given by a fool of a girl who never should have made it."

"A promise is a promise," said Ricky gently.

The Princess was silent for a moment for she knew that a promise should never be broken once it was given. "I was so stupid then," she said more quietly. "You will not try to hold me to a promise that I gave so long ago. Set me free of it, I beg you."

"I cannot and I will not," said Ricky. "I gave you the gift you longed for and in return you promised to be my wife."

The Princess was silent, remembering all the happiness Ricky's gift of cleverness had brought her. At last, she said, "It is true that I owe you a great deal and I could love you for that. But you are so ugly that I would not dare to take you home."

Ricky smiled. "If that is all!" he cried. "Then you, yourself, my beautiful Princess, can change my looks. I have learnt since we met that the wise fairy gave you a special gift as she gave me."

"What is it?" cried the Princess. "Tell me!"

"If you will but love me for myself," replied Ricky. "You can change this ugly creature you see before you into a handsome Prince."

"With all my heart I wish that this was so!" exclaimed the Princess. And no sooner had she spoken than Ricky-of-the-Tuft appeared before her as the most strikingly handsome man she had ever seen in her life.

"Now will you marry me?" asked Ricky, smiling.

"Yes, yes, indeed I will," whispered the Princess. "I now know I could not care for another man as I care for you."

So Ricky-of-the-Tuft and the beautiful Princess were married. They had two wedding feasts; one among the little people of the woods and the other at the Princess's palace where it was clear to everyone that the Princess was marrying the man she truly loved.

Did Ricky really grow into such a very handsome Prince? Some who know this story well have said that it was the Princess's true love for him that made him handsome, and that the wise fairy had very little to do with it . . . but we shall never really know.

The Emperor's New Clothes

THERE WAS once an Emperor who loved new clothes more than he loved anything else in his empire. His greatest delight was to order gorgeous new robes at least three times a week. He spent all his money on his clothes and cared nothing for his soldiers or for the theatre or dancing.

Now the great city where this Emperor lived was always crowded with strangers and many came hoping to see the Emperor wearing something new and very splendid and, of course, they were never disappointed.

One day two rogues came to the city and it wasn't long before they saw a way to cheat the Emperor and win for themselves a great deal of money. "Let's pretend we are weavers," one said to the other. "We'll go to the palace and tell the Emperor that we are the world's best weavers. We'll say the cloth we can weave is the finest ever seen."

The Emperor believed every word the two rogues said when, at last, they stood before him. "Give us gold and silk threads, your Majesty," said they, "and we will set up two looms here in the palace. We promise that you will have a cloth so wonderful that it will dazzle all eyes."

"Certainly, certainly I will!" cried the Emperor. "You will have everything you need to weave this wonderful cloth."

"There is just one thing, your Majesty," said one of the false weavers, bowing low. "Only those who are clever and worthy of their high office can see our cloth."

"Remarkable!" exclaimed the Emperor. "That makes the stuff even more interesting and wonderful!"

The next day the two cheats came to the palace. They brought with them two looms and they set these up in a room specially made ready for them. At their request they were given great quantities of golden thread and the finest coloured silks. They were also given bags of gold to encourage them to work fast.

The Emperor was so excited about this wonderful cloth that he told everyone in the palace about it and how it could only be seen by those who were clever and worthy of the position they held at court. And it wasn't long before all the people in the city knew about the cloth and how only the very stupid would fail to see it.

By the end of the first week the Emperor felt he must know how the two weavers were getting on. "I won't go myself," he thought. "I will send my oldest and most trusted Minister. He is so clever that he will see the cloth and be able to tell me how beautiful it is."

Now the old Minister had served the Emperor for a very long time and he was very proud to be chosen. "I will give you a careful report," he told the Emperor before he hurried off to the weavers.

Imagine his surprise and horror when he entered the room where the two rogues sat at their looms pretending to work, and saw nothing . . . Absolutely nothing, did he see, not even the smallest piece of cloth on the looms. "Gracious me!" thought the old man. "I can't see a thing." But he dared not say so. Instead, he fixed his spectacles more firmly on his nose, and nodded once or twice.

Then one of the rogues said, "The colours and pattern are very fine. You agree, of course!"

And the other said, "Don't you think the Emperor will be pleased? The colours we have chosen will match his eyes!"

The old man was silent for a moment, staring at the empty looms. Then he said, "Yes, yes, very fine. I will tell the Emperor that the cloth you are weaving is truly beautiful."

The two false weavers then began to explain how they had made up the pattern and they told the Minister how much gold thread they had used. "We shall need more gold and more coloured silks," they said at last. "Will you tell the Emperor?"

"I will indeed," said the old Minister, not daring to meet the rogues' eyes in case they should guess his secret.

The Emperor was delighted with his Minister's report. He sent more gold thread and silks to the weavers, which they hid away in a big sack as soon as it arrived.

At the end of the second week the Emperor said that he would go in person to the weavers' room to see if the cloth was nearly finished. He took with him several of his most trusted counsellors and one or two other members of court who were known for their clever, witty remarks.

The two cheats got up from their empty looms and bowed low as the Emperor and his followers crowded into the room.

"Tell us, your Majesty, what you think" said one. "Are you not surprised at the beauty of the cloth and dazzled by the brilliant colours we have chosen?"

"What's this?" the Emperor thought, staring at the looms. "I can see nothing at all! Am I then so stupid? This is terrible. If I speak my thoughts people will say I am not fit to be their Emperor." So he said, "Yes, yes, it is very pretty, quite beautiful."

And all his ministers repeated, "Yes, yes, quite beautiful." For they, like the Emperor, could not bring themselves to speak the truth.

The next day, one of the youngest Ministers spoke to the Emperor. "In two days, the great procession will take place when your Majesty

will walk through the city streets. Will you ask the weavers to finish the cloth and make it into a suit which you can wear in the great procession? The people want to see this wonderful cloth for themselves."

"That is exactly what I intend to do," said the Emperor. And he sent two more bags of gold to the false weavers with a message, saying that they must work through the night to finish the cloth.

The weavers lit tall candles in their room so that the servants would report to the Emperor that they were indeed working all through the night. And, in the morning, they said the cloth was finished.

The Emperor himself hurried to the room when he was given the news and the cheats pretended to take the cloth from the loom. Then one rogue took up a big pair of scissors and pretended to be cutting the cloth while the other measured the Emperor and respectfully asked him how long he would like the train to be.

When the fitting was over, the rogues promised that the suit would be ready the next morning . . . the day of the great procession.

The Emperor rose early and made his way to the weavers' room. Behind him, came two servants carrying a long mirror.

The rogues greeted him with deep bows and respectfully asked him to take off his clothes so that he might be fitted with his new robes. The Emperor did so, and one rogue held his empty hands in the air, exclaiming, "Here are your trousers, your Majesty. They are as light as a spider's cobweb."

And the second rogue exclaimed, "And here is the jacket. Are not the colours dazzling?" And he, too, held up empty hands.

The two false weavers then pretended to help the Emperor into his new clothes and the ministers, who had followed the Emperor into the room, all cried, "Oh, how wonderful they are, your Majesty! How they flatter you! What a perfect fit! What colours!"

The Emperor stared at himself in the long mirror. His eyes told him that he had nothing on but he did not dare say this. Instead, he said, "Yes, yes, they are a splendid fit. Very fine!" And turning to the two cheats, he said, "I will reward you with the title Imperial Court Weavers and see that you have more gold before the procession leaves the palace."

Then his oldest and most trusted Minister, who was in charge of the great procession said, "The crowds have gathered in the streets, your Majesty, the musicians are in their places and all is ready."

Two chamberlains were appointed to hold the Emperor's long train and they stooped down and pretended to pick it up. And the Emperor left the palace and walked down the steps into the street.

"How splendid our Emperor looks today!" the crowd began to shout. "Bravo! What gorgeous clothes! What colours!" No one dared to speak the truth as the Emperor, under the rich canopy, walked slowly by.

Then, suddenly, a little boy cried, "But he has nothing on! Our Emperor is not wearing any clothes at all!"

His father tried to hush his little son but the words had been heard. More children began to shout and laugh. "Nothing on! The Emperor has nothing on!"

Soon all the people took up the cry and many began to laugh. The Emperor heard what they said. Suddenly, he knew that what his people said was true. And, oh, how sad he was and how ashamed! Clearly he had been tricked and cheated by the weavers. But it was his love for new clothes that had turned him into a fool. Still, he was the Emperor. He could not leave the great procession. He must walk through the streets as if nothing was wrong. So the Emperor walked on and behind him came the two chamberlains pretending to carry a train that wasn't there!

The Emperor was never again so fond of new clothes for he had learnt his lesson. But it will be a long time before the people of that great city forget the day of the great procession. And if you are wonder-

ing about the two rogues; why, long before the procession was over, they were galloping their horses out of the city, their bags stuffed with enough gold to last them all the days of their lives.

The Witch in the Woods

THERE WAS once a poor orphan girl called Gertha who worked as a servant to a very rich family. Gertha was gentle and kind and the family liked her so much that whenever they went on holiday they took her with them.

One holiday, the family decided to go for a long trip through the mountains. They were enjoying themselves very much and all went well until they came to a lonely stretch of road with woods on either side. Suddenly, a band of fierce robbers sprang from the trees and before anyone knew what was happening, the robber chief cut free the horses, upturned the carriage and killed Gertha's master and mistress. Trembling with fright, Gertha herself hid behind a boulder and then, when the robbers were looking the other way she escaped into the woods and ran and ran, and when at last she could run no further, she threw herself down on the grass and wept as if her heart would break. She had loved her master and mistress for they were all she had in the world.

But Gertha was as brave as she was gentle and kind and when darkness fell, she dried her eyes and said aloud, "I will stay where I am for there would be little chance of finding the way out of these woods now. Perhaps the good angels will take care of me."

No sooner had she spoken than a beautiful white dove flew down from one of the trees. It had a tiny golden key in its beak and this it put into Gertha's hand. Then it said softly into her ear, "Over there is a great tree and set in the tree is a little lock. Open it with this golden key and you will find something to eat."

Gertha took the key over to the tree, fitted it into the lock, and as she turned it a door swung open. Inside, she found a loaf of white bread and a bowl of creamy milk and she was so hungry and thirsty that she ate all the bread and drank all the milk there and then. But when she looked round for the dove to say thank you, she could not see it anywhere.

Later that night, the dove came to her again. It placed another tiny key in her hand and told her to go once more to the tree. "Open it," the dove said, quietly. "Inside you will find a bed where you can sleep."

Obediently, Gertha went to the tree and using her key, she opened it. Inside was a bed made up with fine linen sheets and it looked so comfortable and inviting that Gertha tumbled into it and fell fast asleep.

In the morning the dove came to her for the third time and for the third time it put a tiny key into her hand, saying, "Do you see that tree to the right of you? Open the door and you will find dresses to wear while you are in these woods."

Gertha obeyed and there, inside the tree, were so many wonderful dresses that she caught her breath in astonishment. "Any one of these will make me look like a Princess," she said out loud. Then she chose a dress of shimmering silver and blue and pulled it over her own shabby dress with its patched skirt. And, oh, how pretty she looked though there was no one to see.

As the days passed, Gertha no longer thought of trying to find her way out of the woods. The dove came to her each morning to see to her needs and although it never stayed longer than two hours, Gertha longed for its visits and in time grew to love the gentle bird.

One morning the dove said to her, "Will you do something for me?"

And Gertha answered, "I will do anything you ask – anything at all, so please what is it you want me to do?"

"I want you to follow me through the woods," said the dove.

"I will take you to a small house where an old woman lives."

"What shall I say to her?" Gertha wanted to know.

"Say nothing," the dove answered. "Do not speak a single word but pass her by on the right side and when you are in the house search for a room that is full of rings."

"What shall I do then?" Gertha asked.

"You must look for the plainest of the rings," said the dove. "You will see many rings that are so beautiful and so enriched with jewels that you will want to try them on. But if you care anything for me you will leave these beautiful rings and take the one that is without a stone and is plain and ordinary. Slip it on your little finger and come back to me here."

"I promise I will do as you say," Gertha whispered, already half afraid of the old woman she had not yet met. Could she be some kind of wicked witch? Before she had time to question the dove further, the bird flew away and Gertha was forced to run after it.

After what seemed a long time and when Gertha was beginning to feel she could scarcely take another step, the dove flew back to her. "Beyond that clump of trees stands the house. I can go no further. Remember what I have said. Take the plainest of the rings and speak no word."

The little house that Gertha came upon looked like any other, but the old woman who stood on the steps was ugly and bent and her red eyes were sharply inquisitive as they fixed themselves upon the girl. "Good-day to you," she croaked. "And what would you be wanting with me? Speak child! Don't be afraid."

But Gertha, remembering the dove's warning, answered not a single word. As quickly as she could, she passed the old woman on her right side and entered the house. Once inside, she ran from room to room until, at last, she came upon a room that was filled with rings.

Never in all her life had Gertha seen such wonderful rings. There were diamond rings, set in bands of twisted gold, that shimmered in the sunlight. Ruby rings that glowed as if they contained a secret fire, and rings set with pearls the size of pebbles. Some were so small they would only fit a child's finger but others were just right for her own slender hands. And, oh, how Gertha longed to try them on!

Just in time, she remembered the dove's warning and, with a sigh, she began to search for the plain, ordinary ring that the dove had told her about. But search as she might, there was no sign of a plain gold band amongst all the glittering rings that shimmered and sparkled on the table and on the chairs.

As she began, for the third time, to search the room, the old woman came to the open door. "Help yourself, child," she croaked. "I am too old for such pretty things. Tell me, which of the rings do you like the best?"

When Gertha made no reply, the old woman hobbled away and Gertha crept to the door to see what she would do next. She saw her stretch up and take a bird's wicker cage from a hook in the wall. And then she saw – and how her heart began to beat – that inside the cage was a small brown bird that held a plain gold ring in its beak!

Gertha sprang towards the old woman, snatched the cage from her hand and opened it. The witch tried to push her away, but Gertha was too strong and quick for her. In a trice, the ring was on her finger and she was running, running, running out of the house and away through the woods.

To her surprise and disappointment, the dove was not waiting for her when she got back. "I have the ring," she thought, "and I have done everything it asked. Why doesn't the dove come to me?" And because she was tired and disappointed she leant up against one of the trees and began silently to weep. Then something very wonderful happened. That self-same tree changed into a tall handsome young man, who put his arms round Gertha, and began speaking to her – in the very voice the dove had used.

"Gertha! My little Gertha," he said. "I am your dove. You have freed me from an enchantment that held me bound for part of the day as a tree and for part of the day as a dove. The old woman was a witch who, out of spite against my father, the King, worked her evil spell on me. It could only be broken by a girl such as you who could find the ring and wear it on her little finger."

Then the King's son took Gertha out of the woods into his father's kingdom where, not long afterwards, they were happily married.

The Elf Hill

IF YOU search long and carefully you may come upon the old elf-hill of this story. It stands close to a wood and not very far from the sea. It is not very tall but it is round and smooth, with a secret door through which the elf maid passes when she has business with the outside world.

Two lizards happened to be near the elf-hill when, one afternoon, it opened and an elf maid came tripping out. She was the old Elf King's housekeeper and she was clearly in a hurry as she ran past the lizards on her way to the sea.

"Something is going on inside the old elf-hill," said one lizard to the other. "I wonder what it can be."

"If we wait around we may find out," said the other. "The elf maid has gone down to the sea to speak to the Night Raven. I'm certain of it."

While the lizards talked together, the elf maid had reached the sea and there was the Night Raven sitting on a stone.

"You are invited to the elf-hill this evening," said the elf maid, "but I want you to do something for me. We shall have a number of important guests and I would be greatly obliged if you would attend to the invitations."

"Who is coming?" asked the Night Raven.

"I have had some argument with the Elf King over the list of guests," said the elf maid. "But it's settled now. The Merman and his daughters are invited. And as they will not be happy on dry land I am arranging that they have wet stones to sit on. We are also inviting the King of the High Mountains, a jolly old gnome who they say is looking for a wife. Our King has seven daughters – all unmarried – so we shall see. And then there will be a number of magicians . . ."

"Croak!" said the Raven, and away he flew to give out the invitations.

That night the great hall of the elf-hill was decorated for the occasion; the floor had been washed with moonshine and the walls rubbed with some special witches' polish so that they glowed like tulips in the light. Mushroom spawn and frogs' legs were tossed into great plates of green salad and there were bottles of deep red blackberry juice and beer for the King of the High Mountains. The Elf King wore a slate crown – very tall and shiny and there was a pleasant scent of burning horse-hair everywhere.

The Elf King's daughters, as they waited for their guests to arrive, looked extremely pretty in their shawls of gossamer which were borrowed from the spiders.

"When will he come, this King of the Mountains?" asked the youngest, who longed to be married and so escape from the elf-hill.

"That depends on the wind and the weather," said the Elf King. "But you'll like him, I'm sure, for he is merry and honest. What's more he has many rock castles and a gold mine. And, he has two sons who most likely will accompany him."

As he spoke, two Will-o'-the-Wisps came hopping up in great excitement. "They're coming! They're coming," they cried.

"Let me stand in the moonshine and welcome them," said the old Elf King, straightening his crown.

The grand old gnome of the mountains wore a crown of polished fir cones and a bear-skin and tall warm boots and very noble did he look as he greeted the Elf King. Then the two Kings went into the elf-hill together and behind them followed the gnome's sons, rough-looking fellows with bare heads and strong arms and legs.

All the other guests were already waiting, and all were thoughtfully arranged. The Merman and his family sat at table in huge washing tubs looking very happy, while the magicians had already begun their entertainment. The Night Raven kept out of the way by perching on a stool.

The Elf King sat at the top of the long table and beside him sat his most honoured guest, the King of the Mountains, who took off his thick fur coat. His two sons took off their boots and put their feet on the table which was not the way true gentlemen should behave, but nothing was said.

Then the Elf King's daughters appeared and danced in a charming way which delighted the old gnome who had never seen girls dance before. "What else can they do?" he asked, for of course he was thinking that he did not want a wife who was only good at dancing.

"You shall see," said their father proudly. "But first let us hear from you."

So then the old gnome told them stories of his mountains; how it was in the winter when the bells on the sledges sounded. And how at certain times, the great salmon leapt up against the falling water, and how waterfalls rushed down over the rocks with white foam and a noise like thunder.

"Bravo!" said the Elf King, when the mountain gnome came to the end of his stories. And he told his housekeeper to bring in the wine and the plates of salad with the frogs' legs and mushroom spawn.

After the feasting, the Elf King presented his daughters, one by one. The youngest was as light and graceful as a moonbeam and she curtseyed low in front of the old gnome, whirled around twice and was gone, completely vanished, which was something she could do very well. But the old King of the Mountains said that he did not think he would care for a vanishing wife. "I don't think my sons would like it either," he said. "After all, she is to be a mother to them and mothers should always be there, not up to any disappearing tricks."

The second daughter fared no better in the gnome's eyes for she was an acrobat and her bending and leaping and twisting in the air quite alarmed him.

"Wait until you meet my third daughter," said the Elf King. "She has learnt the art of cooking from the Moor Woman and knows how to stuff oak leaves and bake delicious mixtures."

"She would certainly make a good housekeeper," said the Elf

King, after he had met her. "But from what she said, she goes in for fancy cooking and my sons like plain solid food."

Now it was the turn of the fourth daughter. She came carrying a great harp and as soon as she struck the first chord, everybody in the hall sprang to their feet and began to hop about. Even the old gnome and the Elf King were forced to jig and hop.

"Enough!" cried the Elf King at last. Then turning to the gnome, who was quite out of breath, he said, "This is her gift. Whenever she plays on her harp, those who hear must dance and jig."

"She wouldn't do at all for me," said the Mountain King. "Quite unsuitable. I have no wish to find myself hopping and jigging whenever she chooses. No, no, I consider her a dangerous woman – What can your next daughter do?"

"I love the mountains," answered the girl, speaking for herself. "I will be safe and happy only if I can go to the mountains with you."

"She only wants to go with you because she is afraid the elf-hill might disappear into the earth one day," whispered her youngest sister. "She thinks the mountains will last for ever . . ."

"If that's the only reason," said the old gnome, "I want none of her."

The sixth daughter would have none of the Old Gnome. "I don't want to marry," she said. "So don't ask me."

Now it was the turn of the seventh daughter. "What can you do?" asked the King of the Mountains.

"I can tell you as many stories as you have fingers on your hands," said she, with a merry smile. And she took the gnome's hands in hers which pleased him greatly. Then she began to tell him wonderful stories – stories of witches and ghosts and Will-o'-the-Wisps and moonshine, one story for each finger.

When, at last, she came to the finger on which sat a broad gold ring, the gnome cried, "Stop! Take the ring. I will have you as my wife. I will hear no more stories now, but when we are home you will tell your stories, for no one in the mountains can spin a tale like you. We shall be happy together."

Then the old gnome and the Elf King's seventh and eldest daughter danced round together and the Merman and his family applauded loudly, clapping their tails against the wash tubs.

"What about your sons?" asked the Elf King hopefully, when the dance was over. "Will they consider two of my other daughters?"

"One wedding in the family is enough," said the gnome, "and

163

besides you can see for yourself how it is with them. They are not interested."

This was true, for the two big boys were fast asleep with their heads on the table. They awoke with the sound of the cock crowing, and the Elf King's housekeeper came in and said, "Now we must close up the shutters, so that the sun will not burn us. The feasting is over. It's time for everybody to go home."

So then the elf-hill opened for the last time and the black Raven who had sat for the most part in a corner, went with the Mer-family down to the sea. And the old gnome and his two sons wrapped themselves up in their furs and left in a hurry, the Elf King's seventh daughter running behind them.

All this was seen by the two lizards who enjoyed every moment of it. "I told you," said one, "that something very strange was going on inside the elf-hill, didn't I?"

"You did," said the other. "And you were right. It looks as if the Elf King has lost a daughter. But then he's got that old gnome for a son. That's what they say, 'lose a daughter and gain a son'."

Then the two lizards, as soon as the elf-hill closed up, ran off to look for their breakfast.

The Sleeping Beauty

THERE WAS once a King and a Queen who longed to have a child of their own more than anything else in the world. Imagine their joy when, one day, the Queen was told that at last she was going to have a baby.

"I should like a little girl," said the Queen.

The King said, "I should like a little boy but what does it matter? Boy or girl, we shall love our baby with all our hearts."

Well, the Queen's wish for a baby girl was granted and she was so lovely, even as a tiny baby, that the King completely forgot he had wanted a boy.

"We must hold a grand Christening Party," said the Queen. "All our friends will be invited, especially the Seven Good Fairies. They will be our guests of honour."

"I have already arranged that the Fairies shall each receive a golden spoon, fork and knife studded with diamonds and rubies," said the King.

The Queen clapped her hands in delight, "And to make it an even more attractive gift we will place them in a gold casket," she exclaimed. "The Fairies will be thrilled!"

On the day of the Christening Party, the palace was crowded with

people all dressed in their finest clothes. The Queen herself was radiant as she invited her guests to take their places at the long banqueting table. The Seven Good Fairies were among the last of the guests to arrive and they were immediately shown to their seats for the Queen was anxious to see their faces when they discovered the splendid gold caskets.

Just as the banquet was about to begin an ancient fairy, with an ugly wrinkled face and a long hooked nose, hobbled into the room. At the sight of the bent figure in the long dark cloak and tall black hat, the guests fell silent. Trembling with rage, the old fairy pointed to the gold caskets set out before the Good Fairies.

"I see no place laid for me," she croaked. "And where is my gold casket? Those who forget me pay dearly. . . ."

The Queen grew pale at the fairy's threatening words. "It is true," she said quickly, "that we did not think to invite you to our baby's Christening Party. We did not remember that you were still in our kingdom. But you are most welcome to sit down at table with us. . . ."

The ancient fairy shook her head. "I will not sit with you," she said angrily. "No place is laid; there is no gift for me. But I will stay. Yes, I will stay and bestow upon your precious child a gift – a very special gift – of my own." and she cackled.

So chilling were her words and so evil was her smile that the other guests could scarcely bring themselves to eat the wonderful dishes that were placed before them. And when the banquet at last came to an end, they hurried into the room where the baby Princess lay in her cradle.

"I must be the very last to bestow a gift upon the royal child," the youngest of the Good Fairies told herself, as she lingered behind the others. "I do not trust that wicked old crone."

Now it was the custom in those far-off days for the Good Fairies to give very special gifts to royal children. They were the kind of gifts that only the Fairies could give.

"You shall have great beauty," said one of the Good Fairies stepping forward and bending over the little Princess.

"You shall sing like the nightingale," said another.

"You shall dance like the wind," said the third.

"You will be gentle and kind," said the fourth.

"And perform every act with grace," said the fifth.

"You will be able to make music on any instrument," said the sixth fairy.

Scarcely had she finished speaking than the old fairy thrust her aside. Bending over the cradle, she bestowed her gift upon the little child: "You will die, die, die!" A gasp of horror went up from the guests, but the old fairy continued, "You will die the day you prick your finger with a spindle from a spinning wheel. . ."

In the silence that followed this terrible curse, the seventh and youngest of the Good Fairies cried, "Take comfort, your Majesties, the Princess shall not die. I have not yet bestowed my gift upon your daughter." And stepping to the cradle side, she said gently, "It is true that I have no power to undo the evil curse. But if your daughter pricks her finger with a spindle, I say she will not die. Instead, she will fall into a deep sleep that will endure for one hundred years. At the end of that time a king's son will wake her with a kiss."

The King and Queen were comforted by the Good Fairy's words and, the very next day, the King sent out a decree which said that all spinning wheels in the kingdom must be burnt without delay. Any person found with a spinning wheel would be instantly put to death.

The Princess grew into the most beautiful, sweet-natured girl that had ever lived. She was loved by everyone and, as the years passed, the King and Queen almost forgot the wicked fairy's threat. No one had seen a spinning wheel for sixteen years or more and the Princess herself had never seen one.

One summer, when the countryside seemed more beautiful than usual, the King and Queen decided to take the Princess to one of their castles in the mountains. As soon as they arrived at the huge, old castle, the Princess immediately began to explore. Up, up, the long winding staircase she ran until, at last, she reached the turret rooms at the very top of the castle.

Pushing open one of the doors, she was surprised to see an old, white-haired woman sitting at a large wheel.

"What are you doing, old lady?" asked the Princess, looking curiously at the wheel. "What is that big wheel for?"

"It's a spinning wheel, child," said the old dame, who had no way of knowing she was addressing a Princess. "And I am spinning. For fifty years or more I have been in this tower busy at my spinning."

"Spinning?" repeated the Princess. "That's a word I have never heard before. But do let me try. It looks such fun!"

"You may try if you wish," said the old woman, smiling at the girl's eager face.

The Princess was in such a hurry that as she took hold of the spindle, it pricked her finger. Immediately she fell to the ground – her eyes closed.

Alarmed and shaken, the old woman stumbled to the top of the stairs, calling loudly for help. Servants came running, crowding and jostling each other in their efforts to be the first to reach the Princess and see what had happened. Some threw water on her face, while others ran to fetch the King and Queen.

When the royal couple saw their daughter lying on the ground, so still and with her eyes tightly shut, they remembered the wicked, fairy's evil curse. "There is nothing we can do," the Queen choked through her tears. "Our daughter will now sleep for a hundred years."

Servants carried the Princess to the royal guest chambers and gently laid her upon a bed of gold and silver.

"She is almost more beautiful now than when she was alive," the Queen whispered, between sobs.

"But she is alive now, too" the King reminded her, gently. "Let us send for the youngest of the Good Fairies and ask her what we should do next."

The King sent his own personal Dwarf messenger to the Good Fairy, knowing that the Dwarf could cover the ground more swiftly than any ordinary mortal. And, within an hour, he had reached the Good Fairy. "I will come at once," she said, when she heard the King's message.

The Good Fairy made the journey to the castle in a chariot of fire drawn by two dragons.

"There is little I can do," the Good Fairy told the King, when she arrived at the castle. "But at least I can make it more pleasant for the Princess on her waking."

Taking her wand, the fairy floated around the castle. First she went down into the vast kitchens and there she gently tapped the cook, the scullery maids, the stewards and the sewing maids with her wand. Can you guess what happened? Each and every one of them fell fast asleep right in the middle of what they were doing. The cook dropped off to sleep with the soup ladle at his lips; the scullery maid fell asleep as she was drying one of the gold plates and the two sewing maids on their stools slept in the very act of threading their needles.

Pages, porters and ladies-in-waiting all slept where they stood or sat. Outside, in the courtyard, grooms fell fast asleep as they brushed

their horses' tails. Even the horses slept. Dogs, cats, hens, and the little birds in the trees were all soon silently sleeping.

When the fairy was satisfied that the whole castle was sound asleep, she returned to the King and Queen. "There is little left to do," she said. "When your daughter wakes up, the castle will come to life again as well and she will not feel strange or lonely."

After thanking the good fairy, they left the castle and rode away in their coach and the fairy climbed into her chariot of fire, drawn by the two dragons. Her task was almost done. Only one thing more must she do before she left. Using her magic powers, the fairy then raised a tangled mass of brambles and prickly bushes all around the castle so that all within might sleep undiscovered and undisturbed.

A hundred years passed. The King and Queen and all the Princess's uncles and aunts were long since dead. Another King ruled over the land and he knew nothing of the sleeping Princess in the woods.

Now this King had a tall handsome son who was very fond of hunting and, one day, while in the woods, the Prince found his way barred by a forest of bushes and brambles.

"What do you think lies beyond this tangled growth?" The Prince asked one of his huntsmen. "For a moment I thought I saw the glint of a castle tower through the branches."

The huntsman shook his head but an old woodcutter heard the Prince's question and spoke up. "Some say an ogre lived in the castle once," he told the Prince. "Others declare it is haunted by ghosts and witches. Who knows?"

"I believe neither in ghosts nor witches," laughed the Prince. "Come, old man, rack your brains. There must be some other more likely tale connected with this place."

The old woodcutter hesitated. "Many long years ago," he began slowly, "My father did tell me a strange story of a beautiful Princess who was left inside the castle, fast asleep. He talked of some wicked enchantment that held her in its power."

The young Prince laughed again. "Here then is an adventure more exciting than a day's hunting," he cried merrily. "A beautiful Princess, you say? Then I will break through this great tangle of bushes and find out for myself."

With that, the Prince drew his sword and prepared to strike a trail through the thorny bushes. To his astonishment they parted before he touched them and there before him lay a winding path through their midst.

More astonished than ever, but still unafraid, the Prince followed the path until at last he came to the castle itself. What a strange and

awesome sight met his eyes. There, about the courtyard, lay dogs and cats sleeping soundly; but it was not just the sight of the sleeping animals that made him wonder if it was he that was dreaming. Grooms, their arms raised as if in the very act of attending their horses, stood there motionless, their eyes shut. An eerie stillness hung about the courtyard and about the castle itself as the Prince pushed open the creaking door.

Everywhere he went it was the same story. "It is true, then," he thought. "This castle is under some evil spell. But where is the beautiful Princess?"

In the last room he went into he found her, lying on a bed of silver and gold and the Prince, as he walked towards her, caught his breath. She was a thousand times more lovely than any girl he had ever seen.

Tenderly he bent over her and kissed the pale face of the sleeping girl. No sooner had his lips brushed her cheek, than the Princess sighed deeply. Then she opened her eyes and sat up.

"So you have come at long last," she whispered softly, holding out her arms to him. "I have waited a hundred years for you."

And as she spoke the whole castle came to life. The cook finished tasting his soup – which was very cold – the sewing maids threaded their needles and stewards and porters rushed hither and thither. In the court-yard dogs barked, cats miaowed and the grooms attended to the horses.

Presently, a lady-in-waiting entered the room to ask if the Princess would like her hair brushed as usual, and the Princess smiled and nodded just as if she had never been asleep.

By the end of that strange day the Prince had declared his love for the Princess and the next morning they were married in the castle's chapel. Never had the Princess looked more beautiful although her wedding gown was a hundred years old!

And at the end of a week of blissful happiness, the Prince told his new wife that soon he must return home.

"I cannot take you with me," he said. "My mother is a strange and jealous woman and would not welcome you. It is best that you remain here in the castle until I judge the time is right."

The Princess willingly agreed for the Prince went on to promise that he would come and see her every day.

When the Prince returned to his home, his mother looked at him with angry, questioning eyes. But he dared not tell her of his secret marriage for he was frightened of what she might do to his lovely wife.

Two years passed. Each day the Prince visited the castle and each day he grew more in love. Now he was the proud father of two children, a pretty little girl called Dawn and a handsome boy called Day.

When his children were about three or four years old, the Prince's father died, and the Prince was proclaimed the new King. Now, he decided, the moment had come when he could safely take his wife and family back to the palace.

From the moment the beautiful young Queen entered the palace, the Queen-Mother hated her. So deep and terrible was this hatred that in time she became more and more of an ogress, possessing cruel and frightening powers.

One day the King was forced to leave his family for his country was at war and the soldiers had asked that he lead them into battle. "I

leave my beloved wife and my two dear children in your care," he said to his mother, little knowing how she felt about them. "Take good care of them for I love them with all my heart."

No sooner had the young King ridden away than the black-hearted old Queen Mother sent for her daughter-in-law and the two children.

"We shall spend the next few weeks in my house in the country," the Queen Mother said. "We shall be safer there."

Almost as soon as the family were settled in a lonely house in the forest, the Queen-Mother sent for one of her servants. "For my supper tonight," she told the huntsman, "I will eat little Dawn."

The huntsman could only stare at the Queen-Mother in speechless horror. For the first time, he saw how long and yellow her teeth were and how she now seemed to be more an ogress than a human-being.

"I cannot do such a dreadful thing," he began to protest. But his mistress cut him short.

"It is your life or the child's," she threatened, and the servant fled from the room.

On his return to his cottage at the bottom of the garden, the poor man confided in his wife. "I love the child," he said. "Since she came here only a few days ago she has quite won me over with her gentle winning ways."

"Then we must think of a way to save her," said his wife, who was a kind-hearted country woman.

At last the huntsman decided what to do. He killed a young lamb and brought it to his wife. The good woman cooked it and then made a tasty sauce, heavily spiced, which she poured over the meat.

"Take that to your mistress," she told her husband. "But before you do, bring the child to me and I will hide her in our cottage."

The Queen-Mother ate the dish with relish that night and the huntsman prayed that it might be the end of the affair. But the next day, however, she sent for him again.

"I will have Day for my supper tonight," she told him, and she looked more than ever like an ogress.

"We must trick her again," said the huntsman's wife. "Bring the boy here and I will hide him."

This time the servant killed a young goat and his wife cooked the meat for many hours in her oven.

Once again, the wicked Queen-Mother was deceived, vowing that she had enjoyed her supper exceedingly well. But, oh dear, worse was to come. She had, so she thought, destroyed the Queen's children. Now she would put an end to the Queen herself, the woman her son loved so much.

"I will have the Queen herself tonight for my supper," she told the huntsman when, once again, he stood before her. "Then, indeed, I shall be at peace."

This time the servant knew that it would be very hard to deceive the ogress, for the Queen, though very beautiful, was more than a hundred years old.

"Our terrible mistress will expect the meat to be tough," he re-

minded his wife, as they talked together later that day. "It is not likely we can work the same trick three times over. This time I must carry out her orders. It is my life or the Queen's." And with that, he grabbed his long hunting knife and rushed from the cottage.

He found the young Queen seated by the window. She was weeping bitterly for she believed that she had lost her two children for ever.

"I know what you have come to do," she said softly. "Take my life. I give it to you gladly for my children are dead and I have nothing to live for." Then she fell on her knees, baring her slender neck.

The kind-hearted huntsman was so overcome by the beautiful Queen's grief that he cried, "Do not weep so, Your Majesty. Your children are alive and well, hidden in my cottage. Let me take you there and I will find some way to trick my evil mistress."

On hearing this joyful news, the Queen sprang to her feet and willingly followed the servant to his cottage where she was reunited with her two children. Then the huntsman went into the forest, caught and killed a young deer and his wife roasted it with such skill that when the meat was ready it was part-tough and part-tender.

So, once again, the wicked Queen-Mother was deceived and after her supper, she sent for the huntsman and complimented him on the way he had carried out her orders. "When my son returns from the wars," she said finally. "You will tell him that a pack of hungry wolves attacked the Queen and the children as they walked in the forest and devoured them."

Who knows what might have happened if the ogress had not, one day, chosen to walk in the garden close to the cottage. Suddenly she heard and recognised Dawn's childish laughter and knew, in a flash, that she had been tricked.

Trembling with rage, her face all shades of black and purple, she had the little family brought to her. Then she had a deep pit dug and she filled it with all sorts of hideous creatures such as snakes, vipers and giant toads. "Now I will see you perish with my own eyes!" cried the ogress.

Scarcely were the words out of her mouth than the King himself strode into the garden. Having returned victorious from the wars, he had come with all speed to find his wife and children. Never again could the ogress hope to deceive her son for now he was seeing for himself her true nature. With a piercing shriek, she turned away from him and cast herself into the deep pit where she was instantly devoured by the waiting vipers.

So, after all, the story of the Sleeping Beauty of the Woods ended happily. The King took her back to his palace, vowing that never again would he leave her and, as far as we know, he kept his promise.

The Robber's Treasure

ONCE UPON a time there were two brothers. One was so rich
that he rode everywhere in a carriage, entertained at his home
twice a week and drank nothing but wine with his meals. But
in spite of his wealth he gave nothing away. The other brother, in
contrast, was so poor that his most valued possession was an old barrow.
In good times, he could afford to feed his wife and children, but more
often than not, he went hungry himself.

The two brothers rarely met, for the rich merchant would not
trouble with a poor relation who was no better than a peddlar. Whenever he saw his young brother in the street, he would look the other way.

One day the poor brother took his barrow into the forest hoping to
fill it with sticks that he could sell in the market. Things had gone
badly for him over the past month and he was worried that he might
not be able to provide for his family. He was so deep in thought, that he
scarcely noticed where he was going until he found himself facing a

tall bare-looking mountain that he could not remember seeing before.

As the poor brother stood there staring at the strange mountain, he saw, in the distance, a company of men coming towards him. "These men could easily be a band of robbers," he thought. So quickly he hid his barrow in the bushes and climbed into a tree so that they would pass without seeing him. When they drew close, he saw that they wore great gold hoops in their ears and colored sashes around their waists in which were stuck long knives. There was no doubt at all that they were robbers and the poor man was thankful that he was hidden.

To his surprise, the robbers stopped when they reached the mountain. Then their leader, a tall fierce-looking man with a black beard and glittering eyes, shouted, "Semsi mountain, Semsi mountain, open yourself!" And at once the mountain opened down the middle. The poor brother could scarcely believe his eyes at this but he counted the

robbers as they disappeared inside. There were twelve of them and when the last had disappeared the mountain closed up again.

Trembling with a mixture of excitement and fear, the poor brother stayed where he was in the tree until, after a short time, the mountain opened again and the robbers appeared, each carrying a heavy sack on his shoulders. When all twelve were outside, their leader shouted, "Semsi mountain, Semsi mountain, shut yourself!" And the gap in the mountain closed. Then laughing and joking, the robbers made off through the forest.

As soon as the noise of their laughter had died away, the pedlar climbed down and ran over to the mountain. "Semsi mountain, Semsi mountain, open yourself!" he cried, trembling with excitement. And the mountain opened.

Oh, what a sight met his eyes as he went inside! He was standing in a cave that was filled with treasure. Gold and silver spilled out of huge brass-bound chests; precious stones, diamonds, rubies and pearls lay in neat piles about the floor and there were, besides, all manner of rich ornaments – bracelets and necklaces such as an Empress might wear.

The poor man gasped, his eyes dazzled by so much splendour. Then, recovering his wits, he went over to one of the chests and began to fill his pockets with gold pieces. When his pockets were bulging, he looked longingly at the precious stones but decided wisely to leave them in their neat piles.

The mountain had closed up behind him but the poor brother, for all his excitement, had not forgotten the password. "Semsi mountain, Semsi mountain, open yourself!" he said, and the mountain opened. Once outside, he said, "Semsi mountain, Semsi mountain, shut yourself," and the mountain closed up once more.

Never had the way home seemed so long as the poor man trundled his barrow through the forest. All his worries were over. The gold would buy food and clothing for his family and there would be plenty to spare for those of his friends who were poorer than himself.

The next few months passed most pleasantly for the poor brother and

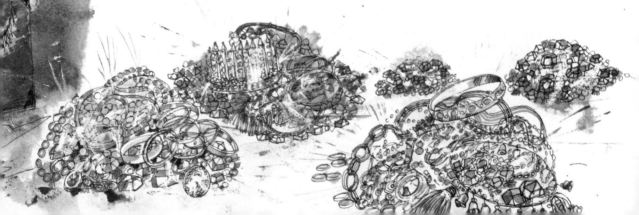

his family. He moved to a bigger house, bought better clothes for himself and his family and was generous to all his friends. He told no one about the mountain except his wife, and it was she who said to him one day, "Husband, we have only a few pieces of gold left. What shall we do when it is all gone?"

"I will return to the mountain," said the poor man. "There is no danger if I keep a sharp look-out for the robbers. They may not even have missed the gold."

"This time take a bushel measure with you," advised his wife. "That will hold all the gold you need and give you an idea of how much you are taking."

Now the poor man did not own a measure and so he went to his brother to borrow one. The merchant was curious to know how his brother had become so well-to-do and eyed his new suit jealously. But the poor man would not answer his questions and finally the merchant gave him the measure.

Once inside the mountain, the poor man took only the gold though it seemed to him that the cave was ablaze with light from the precious stones. When his measure was full, he stepped outside, closed the mountain with the magic password and hurried home. Once again, all went well. Encouraged by his wife, the poor brother bought a carriage and pair and took his family to church every Sunday. Still he did not forget the poor of the town and he made himself responsible for a number of families.

With so many calls on his money, it was not surprising that before long it began to run out. "Borrow the measure again," said his wife. "It is best if you take only a little at a time."

The rich merchant was now green with envy and when his brother called he asked him all kinds of questions in an effort to find out where the money was coming from. But each time, the poor brother answered with a joke which greatly irritated his brother.

"Then tell me," the merchant shouted at last, "why do you want my bushel measure? Has it got something to do with your good fortune?"

"I – er – want to measure some barley," said the poor brother, caught unawares by the question.

"I'll fetch it then," said the merchant, pretending to believe him. But before giving the pitcher to his brother he covered the bottom with tar.

"Now we shall see what sticks to the tar," he whispered to his wife. "I'm certain it won't be barley!"

The pedlar thanked his brother and set out immediately for the mountain. For the third time he was successful in taking the gold without seeing the robbers and thankfully he returned home. Then he emptied out the gold and took the measure back to his brother. But alas, all unbeknown to him, a single gold piece had stuck to the tar and the merchant was quick to discover it.

"Now you'll have to tell me the truth," he said, as he faced his young brother. "If you don't tell me where this gold came from, I'll take it to the justice of peace. For all I know, you may be a robber in disguise."

The poor brother saw that he was beaten and he began telling his story. "Of course, there is no way of getting in or out of that mountain," he finished, "except by using the magic words. Semsi is a queer name for a mountain to be sure, but there you are."

"You were a fool not to help yourself to the diamonds and the rubies!" exclaimed the merchant. "I'll not make the same mistake." And he rushed out of the house.

The merchant had no difficulty in finding the mountain and he was so greedy for the treasure that he forgot all about the robbers themselves. "Semsi mountain, Semsi mountain, open yourself!" he shouted. And the mountain opened down the middle.

"That brother of mine did not lie," cried the merchant when he saw the diamonds, the rubies and the pearls.

So greedy and eager was he to fill the sack he had with him, that he stumbled and almost fell as he reached out to take a handful of precious stones. Working like a madman, he filled his sack to overflowing and then stuffed his pockets until they bulged at the seams. He lost all count of time and forgot everything except the fortune that lay all around him. When at last he was satisfied that he could not push another pearl into his sack he staggered to the front of the cavern and shouted, "Simeli mountain, Simeli mountain, open yourself!" Nothing happened. He had forgotten the mountain's proper name!

In sudden despair, the rich man shouted, "Simeli! Smelimi! Semili!" And a dozen other names but never the right one. His face grew white with fear; he was trapped. His new-found wealth was of no use to him now. Hours passed and the merchant was hoarse with shouting. At last, at the end of the day, the mountain opened and the robbers came in. The merchant cried out in terror at the sight of them and dropped to his knees.

"So we have caught our thief at last!" cried the robber leader. "Now we can take our revenge."

"Mercy!" whispered the rich man, "I did not steal your gold. It was my brother. Set me free and I'll show you where to find him."

But the robbers did not believe him, and really you couldn't blame them, for there was the merchant's sack full with precious stones and his pockets stuffed with gold. And so, being men of action, the robbers cut off his head.

When the merchant did not return, his brother guessed that he had been caught by the robbers. In deep sorrow he sent for his brother's widow and offered her a place in his own home and from then on took care of her as one of the family. Never again did he visit the mountain, but like a wise man, took better care of his gold and with the money from his brother's business, he managed very well for the rest of his days.

The Prince and the Emperor's Daughter

THERE WAS once a Prince who had a very small kingdom. This meant that for a Prince he was very poor. After a time he made up his mind to marry and being exceedingly handsome there were quite a number of pretty Princesses who would like to have been his wife. None, however, was as pretty as the Emperor's only daughter.

Now the Prince was too poor to send costly gifts to the Emperor's palace. But he said to himself, "I will send the two things I value most in the world. My precious rose bush and my own singing nightingale."

The rose bush bloomed only once in five years and whoever smelt the scent of the single red rose became instantly happy. The nightingale sang the sweetest melody of songs in all the world and those who heard it thought they were in heaven.

Certain that the Emperor's daughter would welcome these two wonderful gifts, the Prince put them in silver boxes and addressed them to the Princess.

The day they arrived, the Emperor himself received them and took them into the marble hall where the Princess was playing snap with her maids of honour. When she saw the boxes, she clapped her hands.

"I hope there is a little white pussy cat in one," she cried, "and a long-eared puppy in the other."

But, oh dear me, when the first silver box was opened, there was a rose bush with a single red rose.

All the court ladies said how pretty the rose was and what a wonderful perfume it had. But the Princess would scarcely look at it. "Is it real?" she asked.

"Indeed it is," said one of her maids of honour. "It is the most beautiful rose I have ever seen."

"Take it away at once," stormed the Princess, stamping her tiny foot in its embroidered slipper. "I hate real flowers; their petals fall off and they die. It's a horrible present."

The Emperor looked at his daughter sadly. "How spoilt she is," he thought. "All her life she has had everything she asked for and now nothing pleases her." Then he opened the second box.

The little brown nightingale began at once to sing its charming melody of songs as the Emperor placed its silver cage on the table.

"Beautiful! Quite entrancing!" cried the court ladies, as they listened.

But the spoilt Princess asked, "Is it a mechanical bird – one I can wind up when I want to?"

"No, no, it is a real bird," her youngest maid of honour told her. "And that makes it all the more wonderful. Who would want a toy nightingale instead of a real one, particularly when it sings like this?"

"I would!" cried the Princess, stamping her foot once again. "I don't want it and I won't have it." And she picked up the silver cage and ran to the window.

"Let me have it please." said the youngest maid of honour, who was also the boldest. But the Princess opened the cage and threw the bird into the air. "Go back to your master," she called after it, as it flew away. "Tell him that should he dare to come to my father's palace, I most certainly will not see him.'

News of how the Princess had received his precious gift was soon brought to the Prince. "If the Princess will not see me as I am," he said, "I will go to the palace disguised as a swineherd."

So the Prince stained his face brown and black, put on shabby, patched clothes and pulled a battered old hat down over his face. Then off he went to the Emperor's palace. "It happens that we do need a swineherd to take care of the pigs," said the Head steward, when the

189

Prince spoke to him in the imperial gardens. "The job is yours if you care to take it."

"I'll do my best," said the false swineherd.

So the Prince was appointed the Emperor's swineherd. He was given a miserable hut to sleep in and a hundred pigs to look after. The work was hard and dirty but the new swineherd went about it cheerfully and in his spare time he would sit outside his hut making a little pot with bells all round it. When it was finished, he built a small fire, and placed the pot on top. Then he filled it with water. As soon as the water began to boil the bells rang out in a very pretty way and played an old tune.

Now one day the Princess was out walking with her maids of honour. Suddenly she heard the sound of one of her favourite tunes and it sounded so pretty that she sent one of her court ladies to the swineherd to ask for the pot.

"Ask him how much he wants for it," she said. "Tell him the Princess desires to have it."

The court lady was soon back. "I scarcely dare to tell you what the impudent wretch said," she confessed, almost in tears. "He will not sell his pot for money. He wants ten kisses from you."

The Princess was so surprised that she forgot to show the anger which would have been proper in a true lady.

"What a rude fellow that swineherd must be!" she said, at last. "Of course, a Princess should not think of such things . . ." she broke off, as the pot once again began to tinkle merrily. "But, well, yes I will give him ten kisses if that is the only way I can get the pot."

So the proud, spoilt Princess went to the swineherd and all her maids of honour stood around the pair so that no passerby would see the Emperor's daughter kissing a swineherd.

The very next week the Princess came across the swineherd once again. He had made a rattle that played all the waltzes and polkas and merry jigs imaginable whenever he swung it. As he walked along he swung his rattle and the music it made set the court ladies, accompanying the Princess, dancing and hopping.

"I'll have that rattle," said the Princess, whose own dainty little feet were tapping the ground. "It will amuse me in the evenings and is much better than any of my music boxes."

"Shall I ask him what he wants for it?" whispered the youngest maid of honour.

"Yes, do that," said the Princess.

The youngest maid of honour came back to her mistress with flushed cheeks and bright eyes. "I do not know how to tell you what he said," she confessed. "Something dreadful! He says you must give him one hundred kisses for the musical rattle."

"Indeed I will not," said the Princess. "The impudent fellow has

gone too far." But as she spoke the swineherd swung his rattle and all her maids of honour began jigging up and down in time to its merry tune. "Yet it is truly a marvellous rattle," she went on. "Yes, I will pay the price. But all of you must gather round and spread out your skirts so that no one sees the Emperor's daughter kissing her father's pig-man."

Then the Princess went up to the swineherd and all the ladies of the court gathered round the pair and spread out their dresses.

Meanwhile, as the Princess began kissing the swineherd who was really a Prince, her father stepped out on the balcony. He rubbed his eyes and put on his spectacles. "Now what are those maids of honour up to?" he asked himself. "What new tricks are they playing?"

And he pushed his feet firmly into his slippers and hurried down to the courtyard. He hurried so much that he was quite out of breath, but in his soft slippers he made no sound and the maids of honour were too busy counting the kisses to notice him.

Then the Emperor stood on tip-toe and was so shocked at what he saw that he took off one of his slippers and began hitting the court ladies on the head. "Be off with you!" he shouted, for he was very angry. "Be off with you!"

Then the Emperor saw what he must do if he were to bring his daughter to her senses. "I forbid you to return to the palace," he said. "You are not fit to be a Princess."

Of course the swineherd, too, was sent away. And outside the palace gates, he began to scold the spoilt Princess, telling her that he had lost a good job all because of her. And the Princess began to weep and wish that she had never been born.

"Oh, how silly I am," she sobbed. "I could have married a handsome Prince but I wouldn't even see him because he sent me stupid presents."

The swineherd left her sitting under a tree, crying her eyes out in the rain. Quickly he returned to his hut, washed the brown stain off his face and threw away his rags. Then he dressed himself in a fine velvet suit and looking every inch a royal Prince, even though his kingdom was very small, he returned to the weeping Princess.

At the sight of the tall handsome young man, the Princess dried her eyes and began to smile. "I don't know who you are," she said, "but you look like a Prince and I hope you will take me to your palace."

"That I will never do," said the Prince. "You would not accept my gifts. You did not value the rose and the nightingale that I sent you. You would not even see me. Yet, for a pot with bells on it and a

musical rattle, you were quite willing to kiss a swineherd. I was that swineherd and now I know that you are the most spoilt Princess in the whole world."

Then the Prince went back to his own very small kingdom and, in time, he married a Princess who was just as pretty as the Emperor's daughter and not in the least bit spoilt.

The Crystal Ball

ONCE UPON a time a King decided to build a country house in some woods within his kingdom. But in these woods lived a wicked enchantress. Foresters came to the woods and cut down mighty trees. When she saw the King's foresters fell the mighty trees so they crashed to the ground, the enchantress was enraged. She became determined to seek revenge.

She waited quietly until one day two of the King's sons came to the wood to watch the house being built. Then the enchantress seized her chance, and changed one of the sons into a great eagle doomed to

live in the high rocky mountains. The other son she changed into a giant whale whose home would henceforth be the vast ocean.

Satisfied that she had done the King great harm, the enchantress disappeared for ever from the woods. But when news of the fate of his two sons reached the King's ears, he became ill with grief. After all, his third and youngest son was a gay, light-hearted fellow who was never serious for long. How could the King expect him to wear his crown when he grew too old to rule?

"Do not grieve so much, Father," said the young Prince, when he saw what was in the King's mind. "I will leave the palace and search for a magician whose power is great enough to restore my two brothers to their human shapes."

The King had little faith in his youngest son but he said nothing and gave his permission. The Prince set out at once. For many months he wandered the earth until at last he came to a land where the sun shone both day and night and where everything – the grass, the trees and the flowers – was a golden yellow.

"You are in the Land of the Golden Sun," an old man told him, as he sat down to rest on the edge of a deep forest.

"Do you have any magicians in this wonderful land?" asked the Prince.

"There is one," said the old man. "But he is both wicked and spiteful. Already he has carried off our King's only child, a lovely Princess. Now he holds her captive in a castle among the mountains."

"I will find that castle," cried the young Prince. "I will find it even if it takes me years and years and even if I grow old like you, Grandfather, in my search."

"Many young men as brave and handsome as yourself have tried," the old man warned him. "And none have returned."

The Prince waved and smiled cheerfully as he thanked the old man and set off through the forest. By and by he heard loud grunts and bellows, and he grasped his sword fearing that some wild animal was about to attack him. Instead, he came upon two huge giants with arms like tree trunks, engaged in a battle to the death. So fiercely were they fighting that the Prince saw that soon one or other of them would be killed.

"Stop!" he shouted at the top of his voice. "Surely there is another way to settle your quarrel!"

The giants paused and looked at him in astonishment. "Go away, little man," the red-haired giant roared.

"Not until you tell me what you are fighting about," answered the young Prince firmly.

The smaller of the giants, who had black hair down to his shoulders, pointed to a ragged old cap lying on the grass.

"We're fighting over the cap," he said. "Whoever wins will have it."

"You are surely joking!" exclaimed the Prince in surprise. "That shabby old cap is certainly not worth fighting over."

"Ah!" said the red-haired giant. "That's where you are wrong. It's a wishing-cap and whoever wears it can wish himself away to wherever he likes."

"Well, that does make it a bit special," said the Prince. "I tell you what – I'll put the cap on and go and stand under that great oak tree over there. Then you two must race towards me. Whoever wins the race wins the cap."

The two giants looked at each other. They were both tired of fighting and it seemed to them a sensible way to settle the argument. "We agree," said the red-haired giant. "Put on the wishing-cap and stand under the tree. We'll line up here and when you shout 'Go!' we'll race towards you."

The Prince picked up the cap, put it on his head and walked slowly towards the tree. But as he walked along, he began to think of his brothers and then of the beautiful Princess who was a prisoner in a castle which somehow he must find. And, without thinking, he sighed, "I wish I was in that magician's castle right now."

No one was more surprised than the Prince himself when he found he was standing on top of a high mountain before the gates of a castle that glinted and shimmered in the sun. Then he remembered the wishing-cap which was, of course, still on his head. "I cannot refuse this piece of good fortune," he thought. "But when I have found this spiteful magician and rescued the Princess, I will see to it that the giants have their wishing-cap back."

The Prince entered the castle, boldly determined to fight his way to the beautiful Princess. But every room he entered was empty. At last, at the end of a long passage, he came upon a small room and there inside stood – not the lovely Princess he was expecting – but a bent and shrivelled old woman with a grey wrinkled face and thin brown hair that hung about her face like rats' tails.

Scarcely able to gaze upon such ugliness, the Prince was about to turn away, when the woman cried, "Do not go until you have seen what I really look like." And she ran to him, holding up a small silver-

backed mirror. "Look in the mirror!" she went on. "And you will see a Princess."

Obediently the Prince looked into the mirror and the face he saw there was so sweet and lovely that this time he could scarcely take his eyes away.

"I am under the spell of a wicked magician who lives in the tower of this castle," the Princess told him. "Alas, if you are determined to save me, there are many deeds of courage to be performed. Others who have reached the castle have perished in the attempt. I fear for your life, noble Prince."

"I am ready to do anything," replied the Prince, keeping his eyes firmly fixed on the mirror. "Only tell me what I must do to free you from this terrible spell."

"You must find the crystal ball," the Princess told him. "But first you must leave this castle and take on, in mortal combat, a mighty wild bull. It will toss you on its terrible horns and dash you to the ground unless you find the way straight to its heart with your sword."

"I will fight this wild bull and I will kill it," promised the Prince.

"When it lies dead at your feet," continued the Princess, "a fiery bird will spring out of it. This fiery bird will hold in its claws a large, round egg which is red-hot to the touch. Inside this burning egg is the crystal ball. When you have the crystal ball the magician can work no evil against you. Instead he will be in your power and ready to carry out your commands."

"There are but three things I desire most in life," said the Prince. "I must restore my poor brothers to their human shapes, and I must break the spell which holds you . . ." Then he smiled. "Do not ask me the third. There will be time enough to tell you when all else is accomplished."

Then the brave young Prince, with drawn sword, ran from the castle and down the mountainside. There, at the bottom, a wild bull with long cruel horns waited to do battle with him. Many times the Prince tried to drive his sword into the bull's heart and many times he failed. Once he was tossed high into the air by the bull's terrible horns and once he was almost trampled into the ground by its flashing hooves. But always the Prince returned to the battle.

And at last, after a long and desperate struggle, he plunged his sword deep into the beast's heart. As the mighty animal slowly sank to the ground, a great fiery bird rose from its body and flew upwards into the sky. Watching it helplessly, the Prince saw that it held a huge round red egg in its powerful claws.

In dismay the Prince threw himself down to the ground. Despite the terrible battle he had, after all, lost everything, for he knew that inside the egg lay the crystal ball.

Suddenly, as he looked despairingly upwards, there soared through the sky a huge eagle. The Prince felt his heart begin to beat faster. He knew the mighty eagle was his brother, and he was going to challenge the fiery bird. The eagle swooped down upon the bird, driving it out to sea and striking it time and again with its powerful beak until at last the bird dropped its precious egg into the sea.

"Alas," thought the Prince as he ran to the water's edge. "It has all been in vain, for now the egg is lost at the bottom of the sea." But, how wrong he was! The egg suddenly appeared in a tall jet of water! Then the Prince saw the enormous whale, spouting water, and knew that his second brother had come to his rescue.

The whale cast the egg on to the sandy beach where it lay, red, but no longer burning-hot. The Prince picked it up and cracked it open. There inside was the crystal ball.

Shouting for joy, the Prince ran up the mountainside and into the castle. Up, up a hundred narrow winding stairs he ran until he reached the magician's tower. There he found the magician, crouching over a crystal ball which was clouded and misted over. The magician did not look at the Prince as he burst into the room. But he muttered, "You are lord of the castle, and master of the magicians, now. What do you want?"

"If I am all these things," said the Prince, holding out his crystal ball to the magician, "then I can restore my brothers to their true shape and the Princess to her former beauty."

"It is done, master," said the magician. "Look into your crystal ball."

The Prince stared into his crystal ball and to his great joy and happiness he saw his two brothers walking, arm-in-arm, in his father's courtyard. Then he saw the Princess, her blonde hair falling like gold silk over her slender shoulders, and she was smiling as she gazed into her mirror.

"I want nothing more from you," he told the magician. "Leave the castle immediately and I will not try to punish you for your wicked deeds."

In answer, the magician rose to his feet, and with a fading wail, he vanished in a cloud of dust before the astonished Prince had time to cry out.

The lovely Princess was waiting for him as he ran from the tower, down, down the winding stairs and into her room.

"What is the third desire you spoke of?" she asked shyly, as he took her in his arms.

"To ask you to marry me," the Prince laughed. "And to take you back to my father's palace where your beauty and sweetness will win all hearts."

So the Prince and the Princess were married and in time a beautiful baby girl was born to them. And when she was old enough they told her the story of the crystal ball that always sat on a red velvet cushion in a silver box in the throne room.

"I like it when the two giants were fighting," said the little girl. "What happened to the wishing-cap?"

Then the Prince lifted the magic crystal ball from its silver box and asked her to look into it. And what do you think she saw? She saw the shabby old wishing-cap hanging from the branch of a tree and beside it, two mighty giants, one red-haired and the other black-haired, wrestling fiercely.

"Perhaps you should have kept the wishing-cap, after all," said the little Princess wisely. "Then they wouldn't have anything to fight about!"

What do you think?

The Fairies

THERE ONCE lived a very bad-tempered and disagreeable widow who had two daughters. The eldest, called Fanchon, had the same bad temper as her mother and was both spiteful and lazy, as well. She was especially spiteful to her sister, Rose, who had such a sweet temper and gentle nature that people wondered how they could be sisters.

Well, the widow favoured her eldest daughter. Besides being similar in temperament, Fanchon had another desire that her mother had – and that was to be a grand lady. The widow was not rich but whatever money she had, she spent on Fanchon. She had the best of everything and was so spoilt by her mother that she did no work at all in the house.

Rose, on the other hand, was treated like a servant. She wore her sister's cast-off dresses, cleaned the grates, scrubbed the floors and each morning trudged a mile or so to the village well to draw water. But no matter how hard she worked, she remained gentle and kind.

Early one morning, Rose set out with her pitcher as usual. When she reached the well, she was surprised to find an old woman there. Rose saw how bent her shoulders were and how tattered her shawl and she gave her a sweet smile as she set about filling her pitcher.

"Will you give me a drink of water from your pitcher?" asked the old woman, when Rose's task was done.

"Of course I will," said Rose. "You can have all the water you want. Sit down, madam, rest awhile and drink your fill."

Now the old woman was really a fairy in disguise. So many reports of Rose's kindness had reached her ears that she had come to see for herself if they were true.

After she had drunk the water, the fairy said, "You are as kind and gentle as people say you are. I have not been disappointed. Now I would like to bestow a gift upon you."

Rose, of course, had no idea that it was a fairy speaking and she said quickly, "I want nothing from you, dear lady. No, no, please do not try to give me anything. All I did was a simple kindness."

"And for that simple kindness," said the fairy, "I mean to give you a precious gift. Whenever you open your mouth to speak, flowers and jewels will fall from your lips."

Smiling, Rose picked up her pitcher and returned home, thinking that the poor old woman could not have possibly meant what she said. Her mother was waiting for her at the bottom of the garden. "You lazy good-for-nothing!" she screamed, when she saw Rose. "You've been gossiping, I'll be bound. The fire's out and your sister is waiting for you to clean her shoes . . ."

"I'm sorry, but I met . . ." Rose began and then stopped as sweet-smelling flowers and a shower of rubies dropped from her lips on to the ground at her feet.

Her mother bent down and picked up the rubies only, for the beautiful flowers meant nothing to her. Rose watched her, too astonished to speak, although she remembered clearly what the old woman had said.

"These rubies are real!" cried the widow. "What's all this?" And changing her mind about dealing Rose a slap, she took her arm instead and rushed her into the house.

There Rose began to tell of her meeting with the poor old woman at the well. As she spoke, flowers and precious stones dropped from her lips until every inch of the kitchen table glinted and sparkled.

"You're bewitched, child!" cried her mother, beside herself with

envy and greed as she saw the rubies and diamonds and precious gems. "Why should such good fortune happen to you? Now if only it had happened instead to my dear Fanchon!" And she shouted loudly for her unpleasant daughter to come into the kitchen.

When Fanchon saw the jewels and heard the story, she pinched Rose cruelly and hard out of jealousy and her mother said, "We must think what to do so that you can win a similar gift for yourself."

"Just as long as you don't expect me to walk a mile to the well," said Fanchon. "Such a walk over rough ground would ruin my slippers."

"But that is just what you must do!" cried her mother at last. "To-morrow morning you must take the pitcher to the well. If you see that old woman with the bent shoulders and shawl do anything she asks. Then she'll reward you in the same way as she has rewarded that sister of yours."

The next morning, with her mother's help, Fanchon managed to rise early. "What a nuisance," the girl grumbled, as her mother helped her into one of her prettiest dresses. "You know how I hate walking."

"Never mind," said her mother. "Think of the reward."

"There's one thing, though," said Fanchon when she was ready. "I'm not going to carry that common-looking pitcher that Rose takes. I'll take the silver flagon, then people will know I'm not a servant."

There was an ugly scowl on Fanchon's face when she reached the well. Her slippers were pinching her and the silver flagon had proved heavy to carry. Besides, she was so lazy that any kind of exercise increased her bad temper. To make matters worse there was no sign of the old woman her mother had said would be there. Instead, standing by the well, was a tall handsome lady, richly dressed and with an air of command about her.

Fanchon stared at her rudely and the lady smiled and said, "When you have filled your flagon from the well, will you give me a drink?"

"I will not!" retorted Fanchon. "Why should I? You look as if you could afford servants. I'm not your servant. If you want a drink, get it yourself."

Now the richly dressed lady was really the fairy who had spoken to Rose, though, of course, Fanchon had no way of knowing this.

"You are not very polite," said the fairy, as Fanchon turned away from her.

"What I am has nothing to do with you," said Fanchon over her shoulder. "So mind your own business."

208

"Such bad manners," said the fairy, "deserve one of my more special gifts. With every word you speak, toads and vipers will drop from your lips."

Fanchon paid very little attention to her words. Certain now that the old woman was not going to appear, she set off for home without even filling her flagon with water. As soon as she was within sight of her house, her mother came running down the road to greet her.

"Well?" she gasped, all out of breath and trembling with excitement. "Did you see her? Did she reward you for your kindness?"

"She wasn't there . . ." Fanchon replied angrily, and then stopped, for out of her mouth had dropped three fat toads and three wriggling snakes.

"It's all the fault of that sister of yours," stormed the widow, when Fanchon was inside the house. "No, no, don't say another word," she added quickly, for already the floor was covered with toads and vipers as Fanchon poured out her story. "Just wait till I lay my hands on her."

But when the angry widow began searching the house for her daughter, Rose was nowhere to be found. She had heard and seen all that had happened to Fanchon and she knew that her mother would put all the blame on her and beat her cruelly. Trembling with fear, she put her few belongings into a little bag and fled into the forest.

Too frightened to return home, Rose wandered about the forest

for the rest of the day and then, as darkness began to fall, lay down under a tree. So unhappy was she by now that she could not stop herself from beginning to cry.

Her gentle weeping disturbed the little birds and they flew down to try and comfort her. But for once Rose could take no pleasure in their soft pretty feathers. She sobbed the louder and the sound of her weeping caught the ear of the king's son as he rode homewards after a day's hunting.

His astonishment was great when he came upon the beautiful girl alone in the forest. "Who are you? Where do you come from?" asked the Prince, as he came up to her. "I have never seen you before."

"That is not likely, sire," Rose began, smiling in spite of her sadness. As she spoke, rubies and flowers fell from her lips on to the grass. She stopped immediately but the Prince, recovering from his surprise, begged her to tell him her story.

Well, by the end of it, the Prince was more than half in love with Rose. He had long been searching for a girl as kind and gentle as Rose and to find one whose every word produced a precious stone was wonderful indeed. He took her back to his palace and by the end of the week had made her his Princess.

The news of her sister's good fortune soon reached Fanchon. For very good reason she had spoken very little since the day she visited the well. But now she could not contain herself and toads and vipers hopped and crawled all over the kitchen as she raged on and on.

At last her mother could bear it no longer and she drove the miserable girl from the house, saying it would be best for both of them if Fanchon lived alone for then she would be able to hold her tongue. She was right, of course, and from that day onwards, the proud, spiteful Fanchon lived all by herself in a hut on the edge of the forest and never once did she dare to open her mouth again.

The Flying Trunk

THERE WAS once a merchant, who was so rich that he had enough gold to build a castle. But he did not do so; instead he saved every gold piece he made and when he died he left his only son a vast fortune.

As soon as the son got the money he began to spend it. Every night he treated his friends to drinks and parties and just to show how little he cared about money, he would go down to the river and play ducks and drakes using his gold pieces instead of pebbles. No wonder that, by the end of just one year, the merchant's huge fortune was gone and his son was left with four silver shillings and no clothes to wear but an old dressing-gown and a pair of shabby slippers.

One day, as the young man sat alone in an empty house, having sold all his furniture to pay off his debts, the only friend he had left in the world came to see him. "I've brought you a present," he said. "It's an old trunk. You can pack your clothes in it and set about making your own fortune."

When his friend had left him, the young man thought, "That's all very well. But the only clothes I have to pack are this old dressing-gown and my slippers." And with a grim smile, he climbed into the trunk himself and sat down.

Now the trunk was really a magic trunk. If any one pressed the lock it could fly. Well, it wasn't long before the young man felt sleepy

and as he dozed off leant against the lock. Hey presto! Away went the trunk. Up, up, up through the chimney and over the clouds and on and on, crossing two seas and flying over the tops of several high mountains.

In this way the merchant's son reached the Land of the Turks and having discovered that he could send the trunk down to earth by pressing the catch, he did so. The trunk landed in a forest and the young man climbed out.

Now, as everybody knows, the Turks at that time walked about in dressing-gowns and slippers so the merchant's son had no reason to feel odd as he left the forest and made his way towards the capital city.

Close to the city, he saw a magnificent castle whose only windows were very high up. "Tell me," he said, stopping the first Turkish lady he met on the road. "Who lives in that high castle?"

"Our Sultan keeps his daughter locked up in the tower," the woman told him. "It has been foretold by our star-gazers that the Princess will meet and marry a man who will bring her much unhappiness. The Sultan wishes to protect his daughter from such a man."

"Thank you," said the merchant's son. And he went back to the forest where he had buried his trunk, opened it and climbed in. Soon he was flying up towards the roof of the castle. The trunk made a perfect landing on the roof and the young man was able to climb through the Princess's window.

The Princess was lying asleep on the sofa and he saw at a glance that she was very beautiful. She was so beautiful that he could not stop himself from kissing her.

"Don't be frightened," he said, when the Princess opened her eyes and looked at him in terror. "I am a Turkish Angel. I have flown through the skies to be with you."

Now it seemed to the Princess that the young man must indeed be an angel – how else could he have entered her room? So she invited him to sit beside her on the sofa, and allowed him to hold her slender hands.

The young man was a great story-teller. He talked about big cities where the men wore trousers instead of dressing-gowns, and he told stories of deep rivers and high snowy mountains. He told her about the storks who brought little children to lonely couples and beautiful Princesses who found their true loves among the angels.

Then he said, "Will you marry me?"

And the Princess said "Yes. But you must come here on Saturday. That is the day my Papa, the Sultan, and my Mamma, the Sultana, come to tea. They will be very proud that I am going to marry a Turkish Angel. Please make sure you can tell them a story for they like stories more than anything else."

"I shall bring a story instead of a marriage present," said he, getting ready to climb through the window. But before he went, the Princess gave him a splendid jewelled sword in a sheath embroidered with gold pieces.

With the gold pieces, the young man purchased a truly magnificent dressing-gown covered with stars and dragons, and also a new pair of slippers. Then he buried his flying trunk in the woods, and spent the rest of the week wandering through the capital city, drinking thick, delicious Turkish coffee and eating a large number of tasty meals.

But although he enjoyed himself a lot, he did not stop thinking about the kind of story he would tell the Sultan and the Sultana on the Saturday. "It must be a good one," he thought, "for much depends on it. If I can please the Sultan and Sultana they will surely allow me to marry their lovely daughter."

When Saturday afternoon came, the merchant's son climbed into his flying trunk, flew on to the roof and once again entered the Princess's room by the window. The Princess, her mother and father and several of the court ladies were already there, waiting for him. And, straight away, he began his story.

"There was once," he said, "a bundle of Matches and the Matches were extremely proud of their ancestors. They said they came from a huge fir tree in the forest and that they were much better than anything else to be found in the old kitchen."

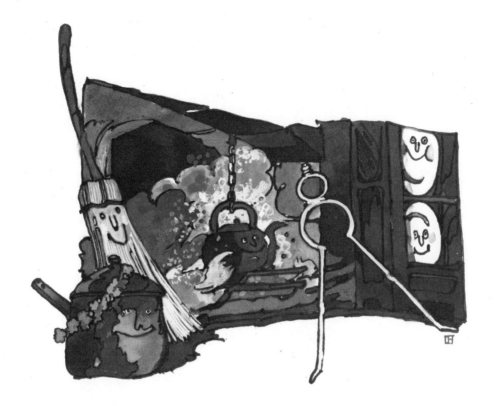

"I don't believe it," cried the Princess, clapping her hands. But the Sultan told her to be quiet.

"The Matches lay between a Tinder-Box and an old iron Pot," went on the storyteller. "When the Matches said what grand people they were, the iron Pot interrupted, saying that in many ways he was also very important. 'I was the first here in the house,' he declared, 'and my greatest pleasure is to sit in my place very clean and neat'."

"I can understand the Pot's pleasure," cried one of the Court ladies, whose mother worked in the palace kitchens. "There is something very attractive about a pot that is well scoured and looks clean and shiny."

"The Matches," went on the merchant's son, paying no attention to the Court lady, "were so proud and thought so much of themselves that they would scarcely listen to the iron Pot as he tried to tell his story. But the Plates rattled with annoyance at the Matches and the Carpet Broom put a wreath of green parsley around the Pot just to teach the Matches a lesson. The Fire Tongs did a dance to draw attention to themselves and the Tea-Pot whistled a song. But all the Matches would say was, 'What common people we have to live amongst'. And then they refused to say anymore . . ."

"Pride comes before a fall," said the Sultana. "Do you know we have a Tea-pot ourselves that sings whenever it is filled with boiling water."

"The Kettle had a better voice than the Tea-pot," went on the

merchant's son. "And just to show the proud Matches what he thought of them, he sang a loud whistling song. It was so loud that the maid heard it and came running into the kitchen. She picked up the Matches and lit the fire with them. And, goodness me, you should have seen how they spluttered and burst into flames! 'Now, you can all see how important we are,' cried the last of the Matches. 'See how we shine!' But then he burned out and there was nothing left of him except a piece of useless charcoal."

The merchant's son stopped and looked at the Sultana. "What do you think of my story?" he asked.

"I enjoyed every word of it," she cried. "It reminded me of the days when I once served as a kitchen-maid before the Sultan fell in love with me . . ."

"Splendid story," declared the Sultan, and all the court ladies clapped their hands. "You shall marry our daughter."

So the wedding was arranged and on the evening before the great day, flags and coloured lights were everywhere to be seen in the capital city. Cakes and sugared biscuits were thrown among the people and everybody wore their most splendid dressing-gowns. It was all so gay and splendid that the merchant's son began to wish that he, too, might do something special to give the people a treat.

"When I was a child," he thought, "I enjoyed a firework display best of all." And he went out and bought a great quantity of rockets and crackers and catherine wheels and other splendid fireworks that gave off showers of golden rain. All these he put into his trunk and then flew up in it over the city.

"Crackle and Bang!" The people in the streets could hardly believe their eyes as they looked upwards and saw the dark sky ablaze with a thousand bright shooting stars. In their excitement children ran up and down shouting, "Hurrah! Hurrah! The Turkish Angel commands the stars to dance for us."

And their parents murmured among themselves, "To think our Princess is marrying an angel. We may look forward to wonderful things in the future."

The next day, in magnificent splendour, the merchant's son and the Princess were married and the wedding celebrations went on from early morning to late at night. At last, when the guests were falling asleep where they stood, the Princess went back to her high turret room, saying, "I will wait for you there," for her bridegroom had said that he wished to be alone for a short time.

The merchant's son hurried back to the forest, meaning to climb into his trunk and fly upwards to his bride. Alas, when he came to the spot where he had left it, he found a pile of ashes. A spark from his fireworks had landed on his wonderful trunk and it had burnt away. Now, he could not fly to his lovely bride who was waiting for him. His days as a Turkish angel were over; and so too was his marriage!

Some say the Turkish Princess is still waiting for her Angel husband but others declare that, after ten years, the Sultana found her another suitable husband. All that is known for certain is that the merchant's son never returned to his own country but wandered through the lands of the East as a story-teller – although never again did he tell the story about the Matches. Most likely he wanted to forget the whole sad business.